A CHRONICLE OF MONSTERS

A FANTASY ANTHOLOGY

RITA A. RUBIN   NICOLE TOTA   TAYLOR HUBBARD

TALLI L. MORGAN   DEWI HARGREAVES

AMANDA FERREIRA   MAWCE HANLIN

AIMEE DONNELLAN   BEAU VAN DALEN

HALLI STARLING

CONTENTS

OTHER WORKS BY

Rita A. Rubin

Of Knights and Books and Falling In Love

Taylor Hubbard

A Corruption of Souls

Talli L. Morgan

Meliora

The Windermere Tales series

The Peacebringer Trilogy

Dewi Hargreaves

The Shield Road

Eyes on the Blue Star

Amanda Ferreira

Entangled With An Elf Prince

Aimee Donnellan

The Chase Begins

The Collection Awakens

Beau Van Delan

The Prince's Dearest Guards

Warrior of Hearts

MOONLIGHT

White; and the colours you showed me

His Darling, Dangerous Count

Android Affection

<u>Halli Starling</u>

Wilderwood

Twelfth Moon

Ask Me For Fire

When He Beckons

A Brighter, Darker Art

The Way We Wind

Always There For You

A Chronicle of Monsters: A Fantasy Anthology

Cover by Juniper Lake Fitzgerald.

Paperback ISBN: 978-0-6450928-8-2

Ebook ISBN: 978-0-6450928-9-9

CONTENT WARNINGS

The Beast of the Greyswood
- — Blood & gore
- — Sexual references
- — Implied past domestic violence

She Sings the Graveyard Hymn
- — Plague
- — Chronic pain
- — Death

Lady of the Dark
- — Violence
- — Mild gore
- — Child abduction

Mightier Than the Sword
- — Blood
- — Mild violence
- — Brief mentions of familial neglect

Oilback Beetle Symbiosis
— Mild animal suffering

We Fellow Monsters
— Fantasy racism
— Transphobia
— References to past child abuse
— Intentional and unintentional misgendering

Atlas
— Violence
— Depression
— Gender dysphoria

Neon Needle
— Mentions of eyeballs

THE BEAST OF THE GREYSWOOD

RITA A. RUBIN

Mattias of Gravende was a Slayer. Meaning, he had been trained since he was old enough to hold the hilt of a dagger in his hands to slay monsters. He spent his days travelling all over Vil Tresar on the lookout for people who had monster problems that needed taking care of and were willing to pay the right price for it.

It was dangerous work, monster slaying. Especially when he was going up against monsters such as foul-tempered gryphons or cunning, blood-thirsty vampyrics. Each time Mattias took a job, he knew it could end in his gruesome demise. But Mattias had long since made peace with that, as all Slayers must. After all, it wasn't as if Mattias had anyone to leave behind.

At least, that *had* been the case once.

"I've never been so far north before. Is it always this cold?"

Upon his bay stallion, Mattias rode through the winding, snow-covered paths of Novicra, the mountainous province in Vil Tresar's north. Riding alongside him on her own horse was a girl of sixteen. She had copper-brown skin—lighter than his own—and hair as black as his, pulled back into a thick plait. Her name was Tsurra, and she had been Mattias's apprentice for a year now.

And his daughter all her life. Though he had not known.

"This is the north," he answered in his gruff rumble. A puff of white appeared in the air as he spoke. "What else did you expect?"

"You know, I'm not really sure," said Tsurra. Like Mattias, she was wrapped up in furs to keep from freezing. "Although I might have expected to see more civilisation by now."

"That's because not many people would choose to make a life out here instead of the warmer, greener south."

"I suppose."

They fell back into silence as they climbed the mountain path. Which was how Mattias preferred it. Since he was eighteen, Mattias had been venturing the world on his own, travelling from place to place in silence. Even after a year, he had not quite grown accustomed to the chatter and insistent questions Tsurra often dealt him.

He first met the girl while staying in the harbour town by the name of Lyancoso, so he could rest and heal from a particularly nasty job with a basilisk. The last time he had been to the small town had been fifteen years ago. When he returned, it was to find a fifteen-year-old girl he had apparently fathered with a serving girl at the tavern. The girl's mother had been claimed by illness some years ago and the tavern's owners had been generous enough to let Tsurra stay while she waited for the day her Slayer father would return to Lyancoso and take her with him.

Mattias had been hesitant at first to take the girl under his wing and bring her into such a dangerous profession. But she was more than enthusiastic enough about becoming a Slayer herself, that in the end, Mattias had relented, and when he left Lyancoso, it had been with Tsurra at his side.

A year later, the pair found themselves in Novicra thanks to a notice pinned to a board in the town square of Razive. The notice had described an issue with people going missing on an estate.

Only to be found dead and their bodies torn to pieces.

The notice also promised a hefty reward for anyone who could take care of the monster dubbed 'The Beast of the Greyswood'. That was all Mattias needed to know before deciding to go and investigate the matter.

By midafternoon, Mattias and Tsurra had passed through their first village. A few yards north-west and they finally reached their destination; the Viencaro estate.

It didn't look much like the kind of estate one might imagine, with elaborate gardens, gilded fences, and an elegant mansion with cream stucco walls.

Instead, the house that loomed ahead of them looked more like a miniature fortress, made mostly from grey stone. The grounds were blanketed in snow, and apart from a few trees with bare branches, there were no gardens or ornate fountains. A low stone fence cordoned off the estate from the surrounding woodland, known as the Greyswood.

It was a dreary and desolate sight. Not a place Mattias would imagine a family of wealth would choose to live. But it didn't matter to Mattias where the rich chose to live. So long as they paid him what he was owed for the job, then they could live in a pig stye for all he cared.

They left their horses out the front while Mattias and Tsurra went to stand at the front doors. When a servant appeared before them, Mattias produced the notice, and they were shown inside immediately.

They were made to wait in the large foyer while the manservant went to fetch Lord Viencaro.

"It's cold here," said Tsurra while they stood in the large foyer.

"Tsurra, if you're going to keep complaining—"

"No, I don't mean the air. I mean, this place. Something seems . . . cold about it."

Mattias looked around at the high, arched ceilings. The tapestries and portraits of past Viencaros all with haughty painted expressions. The spotless floorboards and staircase bannisters. It all spoke of people who lived in luxury—more so than the exterior of the house did. Yet Mattias couldn't help but agree with Tsurra's observation. He wasn't able to put his finger on it, but there was something cold about this house.

Something lifeless.

"Are you Slayers? Here to see my father?"

There was a woman on the staircase in front of them. She was young, perhaps in her thirties. Her skin as fair as ivory, and her golden-blonde hair fell in long, gentle curls down to her waist. She wore a dress of pastel lavender and white lace trim.

"Yes." It was Tsurra who answered. "We saw the notice back in Razive."

"Razive, hm? You must have travelled a long way to get here."

"Obviously."

"Tsurra," Mattias said with warning, and the girl bit her lip.

But the woman only looked amused. She came to meet them at the bottom step. "I believe proper introductions are in order," she said, hands clasped behind her back. "I am Alessendra Viencaro."

"Mattias of Gravende," Mattias introduced himself.

"And I am Tsurra of Lyancoso."

"Your daughter?" Alessendra said to Mattias.

"Is it so obvious?"

"Quite."

Alessendra looked at Mattias with keen hazel eyes and a small smile on her rose-painted lips.

Mattias felt his own lips curving upward.

He pretended not to hear Tsurra's not-so-subtle scoffing.

He did, however, react to the sound of a throat clearing.

Standing atop the staircase where Alessendra had been only moments ago, was an older man. He was broad-shouldered and had a strong, handsome face with slicked back silver hair. Mattias supposed this could only be Lord Viencaro.

"Saints. I think I am already getting frostbite," Tsurra grumbled as she and Mattias wandered through the Greyswood.

If the bite of the northern air was harsh in the daylight hours, it was nothing compared to at night.

"Slayers don't complain, Tsurra."

"My fingers are going all red and swollen. As if I've rubbed them with nipping nettles."

"After we collect the reward from Lord Viencaro, you can use some of those crowns to buy yourself a salve for your fingers," said Mattias mildly.

"That's if we live long enough to collect our reward," said Tsurra. "And don't end up ripped to pieces by whatever monster prowls these parts ourselves."

Mattias smiled.

It had been a day since they arrived at the Viencaro estate and were formally hired by Lord Viencaro to deal with the Beast of the Greyswood. During their meeting, Lord Viencaro explained the first disappearance happened nearly a month ago. It had been their washer woman. She'd stepped out sometime during the night, and a day later they found her disembowelled body outside the front gates. Thinking it to be the work of a pack of wolves, the lord sent some of his personal guards into the Greyswood to hunt them down.

They too had wound up missing. Turning up days later in ragged pieces.

The final victim was Lord Edvichi, an old friend of Lord Viencaro's. He'd been visiting for the day, and his carriage had been attacked as he made his way home at night. Not the carriage driver nor the horses had been spared the carnage.

So far, it didn't seem as though there had been any attacks on the nearby towns. The monster only seemed concerned with those of the Viencaro estate.

"What sort of monster do you believe we're dealing with?" Mattias asked after some time.

"What kind of monster do I think it is?"

"Aye."

Tsurra was silent for a moment as she pondered the question. The snow crunched beneath their boots as they walked. An owl hooted in a nearby tree.

"Well, all the victims were left lying around in the open. I believe we can rule out any gryphons or wyverns, since they would have carried the bodies away to a lair. And trolls don't rip their victims to pieces. They'd eat them bone and all."

Mattias nodded in approval. It pleased him to hear Tsurra make such astute observations about the different species of monsters. She was learning. "Yes. Not to mention, you'd never find a wyvern so far north. They hate the cold."

"And Lord Viencaro said that Lord Edvichi's body had been found strung up in the tree branches like a puppet. So, it must be a monster with a higher intelligence. A ghastly would never make such a display out of their victims. Nor would a diavol or a basilsk. I suppose we could be dealing with a wraith? Or a vampyric?"

"You left out one other creature that could be the culprit," said Mattias, kneeling down by the base of a tree.

"What other monster could it be?"

"A werewolf."

"A werewolf?" Tsurra's tone was incredulous. "But . . . a werewolf wouldn't put their victim's bodies on display. Wouldn't kill discriminately like—Wait. What made you suggest a werewolf?"

"This." Mattias turned, presenting Tsurra with what he'd found by the tree.

It was a clump of damp brownish fur.

"How can you be sure it's from a werewolf?" Tsurra asked.

He held the fur out to her. "Tell me what it smells like."

The girl did as she was told, made a face and said, "It smells like a wet hound that rolled in cow shit."

"And that's how you know it's werewolf fur."

Tsurra gave the fur another disgusted glare. "But if it's a werewolf, it's certainly not killing in the manner that a werewolf normally would, is it?"

"No," Mattias said, "It's not. Which is why I'm sure we're not dealing with an ordinary werewolf."

Tsurra opened her mouth to say more when the sound of something moving behind him stole all his attention.

Whipping around, hand already at the hilt of his sword strapped to his back, it took Mattias a handful of seconds to catch sight of what had made the noise, thanks to the surrounding darkness. But then he saw it. A hunched and hulking figure amongst the shadows. It stood on two long limbs, had a body covered in course dark fur, patched here and there with what looked like mange, and Mattias could see the pale glint of fangs bared in a snarl, and he knew right away. *Werewolf.*

The monster looked at them with eyes that glowed in the dark like hot embers. A deep rumbling growl was heard before it turned and fled through the forest.

Mattias did not hesitate. "*Tsurra.*"

And the two of them were off, chasing after the Beast of the Greyswood.

Werewolves were fast, despite their heavy stature, and Mattias had to push himself especially hard to keep from losing sight of it. Part of him was aware of Tsurra falling behind. Having only had a year's worth of training, her stamina was not yet on par with his own. But Mattias couldn't afford to slow down for her. He had to focus on the target ahead of him.

The werewolf showed no signs of tiring any time soon, and Mattias would not be able to give chase forever. To keep it from leaving his sight, Mattias reached for the dagger sheathed in his belt. He took it out, and just as he leapt over a fallen tree trunk, Mattias sent the blade sailing through the air.

The blade hit its mark, burying itself into the back of the werewolf's shoulder.

With a pained howl, the werewolf lost its footing and crashed to the ground, throwing a plume of snow into the air.

Mattias had not dealt the monster a significant blow, and the werewolf was up on its feet in no time. And this time, instead of running away, the werewolf turned to face him, opening its maw wide to release a deafening roar.

It charged at him; a huge, clawed hand raised. One that could easily cut him to ribbons. Sword in hand, Mattias ducked and spun out of the werewolf's reach.

He moved forward, swinging his sword in a low, silver arc. Aiming for the werewolf's side. With its claws, the werewolf deflected the blade with enough strength that the sword nearly went flying out of Mattias's grip.

The werewolf managed to grab Mattias by his shoulder. Its claws hooked beneath the metal piece there and lifted him from his feet and flung him aside. His back impacted harshly with a tree or a rock, he couldn't be sure, before he collapsed face-first into the freezing snow. Breath stole from his lungs as he coughed and sputtered.

Mattias would have thought the werewolf would have been upon him in an instant. And perhaps it would have, had its attention not been stolen by another.

Tsurra. She leapt down from a rise in the earth. With her own sword drawn, she began battling the werewolf herself, putting all the combat skills she had learnt over the past year to use.

She was good. With more time and training, she would rival even some of the most famed Slayers of Vil Tresar.

The werewolf lashed out at her with its claws. Tsurra ducked beneath its outstretched arm and swung her sword, opening a bloody, but shallow, gash along the werewolf's front. Starting from the top of its ribcage and cutting diagonally up to the corner of its collarbone.

But all the wound served to do was enrage the monster further.

This time, its movements were far too quick and erratic for a novice like Tsurra to hope to keep up with.

First the werewolf clawed a wound across Tsurra's leg, making her lose her balance. It was only for a heartbeat, but it was long enough for the werewolf to surge forward and clamp its jaws around the girl's shoulder.

Tsurra wailed and the sound pierced straight through Mattias. More painful than any physical hurt.

He pushed himself up onto his knees, taking up his broadsword that lay in the snow beside him.

There was no real thought behind what he did next. All that was driving him was the sight of Tsurra in the werewolf's jaws, screaming, and the deep, visceral need to save her. Gripping the hilt of the sword in both hands, Mattias held it above his head, and then, with every bit of strength that he could muster, he *threw* it.

The sword cleared the space between them. Only coming to a stop when the blade pierced straight through the werewolf's left forearm.

The beast let out a horrible cry as it dropped Tsurra from its teeth. It thrashed about and howled some more. Great drops of blood darkened the snow at its feet from where it fell from its wound.

It tried in vain to dislodge the sword from its arm, but only succeeded in widening the wound and spilling more blood.

The werewolf loosed one last frustrated, pained sound, before it turned and disappeared through the Greyswood.

This time, Mattias did not give chase. Instead, he pushed himself with unsteady legs to Tsurra's side.

"Tsurra. *Tsurra*," he called to her as he gathered her up in his arms. "Speak to me, girl."

Her face was ashen, and her breathing laboured. His eyes were instantly drawn to the mangled mess of her shoulder. Her neck and even her face were stained with the blood, and he could already feel it soaking into his own clothing where he held her.

Fuck. The worst thing that could happen to a Slayer when going up against a werewolf—other than dying—was being bitten. A bite was how the affliction passed from one poor soul to another. Already, it would be working its way through Tsurra's blood. Turning her into a monster.

Tsurra whimpered.

Unless, of course, the wound didn't kill her first.

Mattias gritted his teeth. "Hold on, Tsurra." He hoisted her up as he rose to his feet. "I've got you . . . I've got you."

It didn't take long to fetch the doctor from the nearby town. But for Mattias, it felt as if it took an age.

The Saints must have decided to lend Mattias their favour that night, because the doctor also happened to be a sorcerer. The old man was able to use the magic from his emerald serpent amulet to halt Tsurra's blood loss, and then replenish some. Mattias stayed seated at Tsurra's bedside, opposite the doctor. Watching as the man cleaned and stitched the wound in Tsurra's shoulder.

Tsurra's eyes remained closed throughout all of it. She was so pale, and the sight still made Mattias feel as though a shard of glass was lodged in his heart.

"It's a dreadful wound," the doctor told him by the bedroom door after he had finished his work, "but with enough time and rest, I believe she will be on the mend."

"Thank you. For all your help," Mattias said.

"Also, you said that the wound came from a werewolf bite. Yet when I was healing her with my amulet, I did not sense the disease in her blood. Perhaps it is simply still too early to tell, but I thought I should let you know."

No disease in her blood? That couldn't be possible. But Mattias didn't voice this. Only bid the doctor goodnight.

For the next few days and nights, Mattias stayed by Tsurra's bedside. Changing the dressing on her wound, making sure she ate and drank water in the moments when she was awake. He also watched over her for any signs that she was changing. That she was turning into one of the things he was born and bred to slay.

One night, Mattias dreamt that he walked into her room to find Tsurra gone and a werewolf in her place. And when it attacked, he did not reach for a weapon. Did not try to defend himself. Only let Tsurra's claws tear straight through his heart. He'd awoken with a jolt to find Tsurra still in bed. Still sleeping and still human. Blissfully oblivious to the turmoil churning like a storm within Mattias. Brought on by the realisation that he might not be able to end his daughter's life, even if she did become a monster.

After the fourth day, however, Tsurra still showed no signs of turning. And Mattias didn't know whether to feel relieved or perplexed.

A person normally succumbed to lycanthropy within three days of being bitten. There were records of it taking longer, four or five days, but it was unheard of for one to go four days without exhibiting any kind symptoms.

He almost believed this anomaly was because of Tsurra. That the girl had some never-before-seen immunity. Except . . .

"I'm sure we're not dealing with an ordinary werewolf."

During the time Tsurra spent recovering and Mattias spent watching over her, there had been no more attacks and no sightings of the werewolf. Lord Viencaro was delighted by this, having taken it to mean that the monster was gone for good. He'd even gone so far as to pay Mattias the reward in full.

Mattias supposed it was entirely possible that the werewolf had decided to flee these parts after its encounter with Tsurra and himself.

And yet, Mattias found it difficult to believe.

So, as Tsurra slowly but surely mended, and he felt more comfortable leaving her side, Mattias patrolled the Greyswood at night. Looking for any sign that the werewolf was still around. Yet each time, he found none. He even discovered a shallow cave deep in the forest that looked like the perfect place for a werewolf den. But still, there was nothing. Not even the horrible smell of wet and shit.

However, he did find his sword. The blade covered in brownish blood that looked as if t had dried days ago.

It looked like the werewolf really had vanished.

So why did Mattias have such a strong feeling otherwise?

When Mattias returned to the mansion that night, he did as he always did, and made straight for Tsurra's room. It was well into the night, and he expected to find her asleep. Instead, he found the candlestick still lit where it stood on the bedside table, Tsurra sitting up in bed, and Alessendra Viencaro sitting in the chair Mattias normally occupied.

The pair of them were speaking and laughing softly with each other.

"Am I interrupting?" said Mattias.

"I couldn't sleep," Tsurra explained, "And Lady Alessendra offered to keep me company for a bit. She's been telling me stories and even made me a cup of warm milk."

It was only then that Mattias noticed the book in Alessendra's lap. "I've been confined to bed these last couple of days. As happens every month." A wry smile touched her lips and Mattias averted his eyes, her meaning clear. "So, I felt guilty about not paying a visit to Tsurra and thought I would make up for it tonight."

"I enjoyed the story you told about the sorcerer turning her cheating lover into a pig," Tsurra said.

"That one was my favourite as a girl as well."

Tsurra smiled more broadly than she had in days. Though drowsiness dampened it somewhat.

Alessendra rose from her seat. "I think I've kept you awake long enough. I shall let you sleep."

"I'll walk you back to your room," Mattias offered, since the room they had given him was further down the hall from Alessendra's.

They bid Tsurra goodnight, and together, set off through the night-darkened corridors. The candlelight in Mattias's hand guiding their way.

"That was nice of you," said Mattias. "To read to Tsurra."

"She seemed quite taken with the stories. It reminded me of when my mother would read to me when I was close to Tsurra's age."

Mattias studied the book Alessendra held close to her chest. It was bound in worn, cracked leather. The pages yellowed. "Is the Lady Viencaro . . ?"

"Dead?" Alessendra finished for him. "Yes. For almost thirteen years now."

"I'm sorry."

"As am I. My mother was a remarkable woman. Gone far before her time."

They were traipsing up a small flight of stairs now. The steps creaking under Mattias's feet, but not Alessendra's much lighter tread.

"At least you still have your father to keep you company," Mattias said.

There was a pause before Alessendra finally said, "Lord Viencaro is my mother's second husband. They married a few years after my real father died in a hunting accident."

This came as a surprise to Mattias. He had noticed the complete lack of any physical similarities between Alessendra and Lord Viencaro, but he had thought little of it. After all, Tsurra bore a striking resemblance to himself, while looking very little like her mother.

They came to a stop outside the closed door to Alessendra's bedroom.

"Well," he said, "goodnight, My Lady."

She smiled up at him. "Goodnight, Master Slayer."

As she made to turn away from him, the book slipped out of her hold and landed with a soft thud on the carpeted floor.

They both reached to retrieve it at the same time. Their fingers just shy of touching each other's. Only when Mattias looked up did he realise how little space now existed between the two of them.

They stilled. A stretched-out moment where they simply gazed at one another.

In the candle's glow, Alessendra's eyes had turned the colour of honey. He could see a hint of perfect white teeth from between her parted lips. Alessendra's beauty hit him like a soft blow to the chest. It wasn't often Mattias found himself drawn to women the way he was drawn to men. The last woman to spark this feeling of desire in him was Tsurra's mother, sixteen years ago.

It was Alessendra who leaned forward. Mattias was unable to do anything but let her lips touch his in a slow, deliberate kiss. As light as a moth's wing, but no less alluring.

When Alessendra pulled back, she lifted her lashes to study his face, as if to make certain her advance had not put him off.

The expression on Alessendra's face was intent. Mattias could tell that she wanted this—wanted *him*—even before she said, "Come into my rooms?"

He didn't hesitate. "Yes."

And he let her guide him through her door.

Later, they lay naked and sated together on the rumpled sheets of Alessendra's bed. The fire in the room had gone out long ago, yet they both felt perfectly warm.

Alessendra rested her head against Mattias's chest, idly petting the black hairs there. Their figures were bathed in the silvery moonlight that spilled in from the tall windows in the wall beside the bed.

Mattias watched Alessendra's hand on his chest and noticed the shiny slice of scar tissue below her wrist bone.

"You have a scar," he noted.

"And you have many," Alessendra responded, running her fingertips over one on his abdomen. It was a diagonal slash, given to him by the horn of a diavol—enormous monsters that looked like a grotesque combination of a bear and a deer.

"It comes with the occupation," said Mattias. "I had meant to ask you something."

"Yes?"

"How have you been coping with a monster prowling so close to your home?"

Alessendra was silent, and for a moment Mattias wondered if she would answer him at all.

"The monster has concerned me little," she said.

Mattias looked at her, disbelieving. "A creature who has killed your staff and friends of your father's doesn't concern you?"

"The monsters with sharp teeth and claws do not frighten me, Master Slayer. I believe the monsters who look like us and call themselves men are much more frightening."

Mattias came awake with a start. A scream rang in his ears.

He wasn't sure whether it was merely the remnants of a dream, or whether he really had heard it. What Mattias did know was that he had the keen feeling that something was wrong in this house.

It also didn't take him long to realise that he was alone in the bed. That the room was empty except for him, and the bedroom door was ajar, letting in a cool draft that only increased his sense of foreboding.

Mattias dressed quickly. Taking with him his sheathed sword that he hadn't had a chance to remove after returning to the estate, he stepped out into the hallway. He saw no one and heard nothing but the eerie sound of the wind blowing outside. Even as he made his way through the halls, nothing seemed amiss.

He made it to Tsurra's room, and his relief when he saw her still in bed was a palpable thing.

"Tsurra." He gave her uninjured shoulder a shake. "Tsurra, wake up."

But she wouldn't wake. Only made a drowsy sound that at least assured him she was still alive.

Mattias frowned to himself. Tsurra was never so difficult to rouse. He cast his gaze to the bedside table and the now empty cup of milk. She said Alessendra had given it to her.

Mattias lifted it to his nose and immediately caught a lingering scent that reminded him of spice and lavender. It was faint, however. So much so that Tsurra never would have known the milk she had drank was laced with lulling poppy. A flower seed that once broken and ingested would put one into a deep sleep. It was often used when performing surgery and to treat insomnia.

So, at the very least, Mattias could rest assured that Tsurra was fine and would wake again in a few more hours.

A muffled noise startled him. Like something heavy falling to the floor. It sounded as though it came from the upper floor.

With no choice but to leave Tsurra as she was, Mattias raced toward the staircase at the end of the hall.

When he made it to the top floor, again, there were no obvious signs that something was wrong. But Mattias knew that something was, because clinging to the air was the unmistakable, coppery scent of blood. And he knew that for the smell of it to be this powerful, much blood must have been spilt.

He cautiously made his way down the hall, keeping his steps light and his sword at the ready. His eyes darted from one shadowy corner to the next. His ears trained for even the slightest sound.

All the doors Mattias passed were closed, except for the one straight ahead of him, at the very end of the hallway. He eased himself through the half-open door . . . and came to a halt.

He was standing in an over-large bedroom, illuminated by shafts of moonlight coming in through the arched windows. At the front of the room, across from Mattias, was a wide, canopied bed, draped with embroidered rugs and cushions.

Lying on the floor at the foot of the bed was the mangled body of Lord Viencaro, lying in a pool of his own blood. From the neck down, he looked as if he had been hacked apart by an unskilled butcher.

Mattias could even see a few innards and the tips of white bones from the man's ribcage.

But that wasn't the only thing that made Mattias go still.

The smell hit him before he saw it. That awful stench of wet dog and excrement.

For standing by the side of the bed, taller even than the canopy, was the werewolf. Blood coating nearly every inch of it. Blood that was surely from the body of Lord Viencaro.

It growled low, baring its bloodied fangs at him in a snarl, and that was all it took to launch Mattias into action.

He darted across the room, the point of his blade ready to sheer through the werewolf's body.

But of course, the werewolf side-stepped him. Hitting him in the ribs hard enough that he lost his footing and wound up on his back, temporarily winded.

Before he could even think of moving, the werewolf pounced on him, keeping him pinned to the floor.

Mattias managed to free his sword arm, however. He swung the blade towards the beast's neck, and the werewolf caught the sword in its own hand. The blade cut deep into its palm, spilling fat droplets of blood.

The monster roared, foul breath and spittle flying into Mattias's face. It stared down at him with eyes alight with rage. Yet instead of doing to him what it had done to Lord Viencaro, Mattias noticed something starting to change in the werewolf.

At first, he thought it was convulsing, then he heard an audible snapping of bones as its back contorted and its limbs began to shorten. He saw the black fur along its body fall away and realised that the werewolf was shifting back to its original form.

After a handful of gruesome moments, Mattias no longer had a werewolf standing over him, but a woman with long golden hair.

"Alessendra?"

Alessendra Viencaro stood as bare as she had been in bed with him only a short while ago. Her normally immaculate hair was in tangled disorder, with some of it falling over her face. Dark blood stained the lower half of her face and much of the front of her body and both arms, as it had in her werewolf form.

Still, she smiled at him, and it wasn't a pleasant thing. "Be at ease, Mattias of Gravende. I don't intend to shed any more blood tonight. Unless you give me a reason."

Mattias was torn between slicing through Alessendra's hand to get to her neck, and demanding answers. He settled on the latter.

"You've been the monster this whole time?" he said. "You killed those people?"

Alessendra uncurled her hand from his blade, seemingly uncaring about the ragged wound it left in her palm and stepped back. "Yes. I was always the Beast of the Greyswood."

Mattias pulled himself to his feet, not releasing his grip on his sword. "You bit Tsurra. You almost killed her," he growled.

"I am sorry about that." Mattias thought he saw a flicker of remorse cross her face. "Sometimes the beastly nature is hard to control when I take on that form. I never intended to kill anyone I hadn't already planned to. Not even you, the Slayer, hired to kill me."

"Clearly there is a story here I am not yet privy to. So, explain, before I decide to fulfil my end of the contract after all."

"I told you about my mother," Alessendra began. "That she died thirteen years ago. What I didn't mention was that she did not die from natural causes. She was murdered. By *him*." She cast a baleful glare at the body lying behind her.

"Lord Viencaro?"

"He had mistreated her for years. For years, I did nothing but watch on as he verbally degraded her, beat her, and worse. Until one day she had enough. Told him she would end their marriage and cast him from this house. But he refused to let that happen. Better to be a widower than have his wife throw him out. So, he killed her, and told everyone she had done it to herself."

Mattias might have been mistrustful of such a story without anything to prove it if not for the very real emotion behind Alessendra's words. Such grief and hatred could not possibly be born from a false tale.

"And yet you never said anything otherwise and continued to live under the same roof as your mother's killer?"

"I was a stupid, fearful girl," said Alessendra with disgust. Disgust at herself. "I never spoke a word or lifted a finger to protect my mother, because I was scared my stepfather would hurt me. And after my mother died, I worried that he would kill me too, if I ever spoke out against him or tried to run away."

"Why would a werewolf fear an ordinary man?"

"I was not always a werewolf. This curse is one I only came to bear many months ago. Thanks to the help of a strega I encountered while wandering the Greyswood one evening. She told me she could sense a great well of rage and sorrow within me, so I told her about my mother. I told her I wished I could be strong enough to avenge her. And the strega granted my wish. She gave me the power to take revenge upon my stepfather by turning me into a monster for one year. A monster that would make even him quake in fear."

So that was why Tsurra did not turn after being bitten, Mattias thought. *She's only a werewolf through some spell, not by the disease. And only a temporary one at that.*

"So you wanted to kill your stepfather for murdering your mother," he said. "I can understand that. But what about all the others? The washerwoman? Lord Edvichi?"

"My revenge wasn't just about murdering my stepfather and being done with it," Alessendra explained. "I wanted him to feel even just a fraction of the fear he instilled in me for all those years. Killing the washerwoman who was his mistress even while my mother was still alive, and his dear friend, who cornered me in the corridors on more than one occasion, seemed like a good way to unnerve him."

Mattias considered Alessendra, standing before him. A woman cursed by a monster's magic to turn into a monster herself. A woman who had done horrific things to the humans Mattias was supposed to protect. With her hair in disarray, the blood of her stepfather covering most of her pale skin and a dark look upon her face, Mattias thought she could even be mistaken for a vampyric or a wraith in that moment.

His gaze slid from Alessendra to the body of Lord Viencaro, his blood still seeping into the carpets. He had died a gruesome death, but after what Mattias had just heard, it sounded as if he had deserved no less.

A dreadful death for a dreadful man.

A monstrous man.

"So, you've heard my tale," Alessendra said. "What will you do now, Master Slayer?"

The gardens at the temple of Siarella—the Saint of Healing—were quiet and peaceful, filled only with the sound of birdsong and the gentle rushing of water from a nearby fountain.

Mattias sat on a stone bench beneath the sun-dappled shade of an azalea tree, enjoying the solitude.

He had been at the temple for almost two weeks now, as Tsurra recovered from her wounds.

They had left the Viencaro estate the same night Mattias learned the sordid truth of the Lord of the manor and Alessendra. Left the torn body of Lord Viencaro bleeding on the floor. Left Alessendra alive, despite each of his Slayer instincts telling him to kill her where she stood.

He'd left the room, gathered their things and brought the still sleeping Tsurra down to the stables where their horses awaited them and rode out the gates.

Mattias had wondered in the days since if he had done the right thing, in leaving Alessendra alive. What if her curse wasn't temporary? What if she decided she wasn't finished killing?

Had it been foolish of him to take her at her word?

"I thought I might find you out here."

Mattias saw Tsurra walking down one of the garden pathways to come and join him on the bench.

"Did you need some time alone to brood?" she asked him. Her hair was loose and damp—likely from a bath—and she was dressed in a plain tunic and trousers.

"Not brooding," said Mattias. "But I was looking for some alone time. A shame that's now come to an end."

"Just pretend I'm not even here."

"How could I possibly?"

Tsurra grinned. The silence between them only lasted a few moments before she spoke again.

"So, when are we going to get back on the road?"

Mattias looked at her carefully. "Do you feel healed enough to leave? There's no rush. We can stay here for a while longer if you need."

"I feel fine," said Tsurra. "And the sisters said I'm healed enough to travel again." A mischievous glint entered her eye. "Or do you simply want to stay for that handsome, blond-haired serving man?"

Mattias shot her a reproachful glare, and her expression wilted.

With a chuckle, Mattias reached out and mussed her hair.

Tsurra complained and pushed his hand away.

Mattias looked to the blue sky above them in time to see a pair of swallows fly overhead. For all its tranquil beauty, the temple walls were beginning to stifle Mattias. And he felt a sudden ache of longing for the saddle and the never-ending road ahead of him.

"When do you want to head off?"

SHE SINGS THE GRAVEYARD HYMN

NICOLE TOTA

I knew by the song in the air that death was near.

It was a lilting tune, mournful enough to break even the hardest of hearts, and I was no hardened cynic, but a tender-hearted healer. I kept my hands tightly clasped, my eyes fixed upon the sickbed, my magic coiled in waiting, as Dr. Rathbone pulled leeches from our patient's arms. The wet suction of them echoed throughout the room. Even before they slithered back into their jar, I knew what he would ask of me.

I held out my hands. He placed the jar into them, his palms dusty like a moth's wing, but fingers leech-slick. His cool gray eyes met mine.

"Catriona," he said. "I've done all I can do."

And then he stepped aside. I did not tell him that our patient was a lost cause, for how could I confess to hearing banshee song, when it took a display of great faith three years ago to even convince him that my powers were true?

I nodded and said, "I will try, Doctor, but I give no guarantees," as outside the soot-stained window, the banshee howled. The leeches, now resting upon the sill, clambered up the jar's side as if pulled to escape.

When I placed a hand upon our patient's clammy brow, I felt the dying spasms of her soul. When I pressed my fingers against her wrist, the veins black and bulbous beneath papery skin, it was like touching a leather satchel, a book, a pressed flower. Something that once came from life and yet little resembled the living. I glanced outside the window, where a white light danced between speckles of tar, then at the expectant Dr. Rathbone. If I refused to heal her, I would have disappointed him twice tonight, a dangerous thing for a woman whose position was as tenuous as mine.

Yet, if I dragged out this patient's death—who, by the purplish-black eggs of her lymph nodes and shallow rasps of her breath, should have been gone hours ago—I set myself up for a painful night. My healing magic was not truly a gift, though surely everyone who paid for Dr. Rathbone's services thought so. For them, it was a month's wages and a near-guarantee of full recovery from any injury. For me, it was a trade: if I gave up some of my life force to heal another, my own body would protest the loss. My joints would crack and swell for days, my muscles aching around them, so that nightly rounds with Dr. Rathbone would feel like a three-day trek up the mountains.

Last week had not been easy, but my duties had been mild enough that I only hurt when I thought too deeply about it. But if this patient was a herald of things to come, today was to be my last pain-free day for months.

"Well?" He asked, as a cough in the doorway drew my attention. A concerned woman, only a few years younger than me, her fingers white-knuckled against the splintered wood.

"It's not working tonight," I said.

A frown deepened his already-wrinkled brow. In the doorway, the woman turned a shade paler, swaying on unsteady feet as the good doctor placed a reassuring hand on her arm. "It will. It may just take some time tonight before her magic can—"

I shook my head, cutting him off with a new boldness, or perhaps a simple desire to leave. "This is not an ordinary fever, Doctor. We both know this. If I could heal plague, perhaps I would still have my mother."

In the doorway, a sharp gasp and shriek, an anguished cry, "You said you could save my sister!"

On the sickbed, our patient's lids fluttered shut. I ghosted my hand over her mouth, feeling a last breath puff against my palm. I crossed her arms over her chest, pulled the sheet overtop, and wiped my hands against my skirt, while I waited for Doctor Rathbone to finish. Meanwhile, the banshee's lament drew nearer.

And when he was done, mercifully soon, I helped him pack his leech jar and bloodletting bowl, his stained scalpels and sachets of herbs, and I gathered his hefty doctor's bag into my arms. If a housecall went well, he'd hold the door open for me, waiting for me to step through with a gentle bow that I supposed he thought was charming. Tonight, he let it swing shut behind him, stopped only by my kneecap as I jammed my leg into the opening. I swore softly under my breath.

"You should not have called it that," he said, once I finally hobbled through. "The plague."

"It is the truth, though. Would you prefer that I lied?" I asked, setting his bag down onto our carriage with a groan, the weight nearly pulling me forward.

He stopped midway between the carriage and door, a tub of red paint and a brush dangling from his fingers. "I would prefer that you not use that term. It'll only spread hysteria for what is bound to be an isolated case. Look around you, Catriona. We're far from civilization."

It was true. Tonight's call was an hour's journey from town, a small cottage hidden within acres of pine forests. The ride had been treacherous, our horse's legs cut to bits by brambles. If we hadn't needed the money after a rough month, I doubt we'd have come at all. But I didn't want to agree with him. I felt small, like a chastised child, in the face of his condemnation. I cast my eyes towards the pines as the slap of paint on the splintered door mingled with the cry of death.

The keening was louder out here, more insistent, her white light blinding. I filled my ears with it, while Doctor Rathbone's words droned into the night air like a mosquito. I sought glimpses of her through the trees, chasing the light down with my eyes until she crystallized into life.

And then, I could not breathe.

She was young, my age, with her moonlight-white hair billowing around her in an unseen breeze. White veil trailing beneath her bare feet. Pale lips open in a wordless song. Her eyes locked onto mine, and it was as if there were a thread unspooling between the two of us, from my heart straight into the ether. Perhaps that should have frightened me, but all I felt was a white-hot yearning. She paused. I held my hand out tentatively; she mirrored me, and there we stood for endless seconds, before a thick sigh drew me back to myself.

"You seem distracted," Rathbone said, as he wiped the last drippings from the red cross he'd painted on the door beneath the words, *Lord have mercy on us.*

What was I to say? That the call of the banshee's song was like a balm for my wounded soul, and I wanted nothing more than to sprint after this deadly creature? He'd think I'd gone mad. The banshee were legends, stories spun to terrify travelers on long, isolated nights in the hinterlands, and easily dispelled as the jagged screams of foxes. Almost no one believed, truly believed, that ghostly women would show up outside the cottages of the dying to herald them into the afterlife. But then, no one believed in my healing magic, either, until I placed my hands upon them.

Some things defied mortal explanation.

But Dr. Aldous Rathbone was mortal through and through.

"I am thinking of my mother and her untimely death," I said, by way of explanation.

"Ah. Well, may God rest her soul." He folded his supplies back into the bag I'd just lugged onto the carriage, pulling himself up onto the driver's seat. "In any case, have you thought about my proposal?"

I did not answer as I clambered up beside him, my knees creaking in protest. I could not bear to look at him. Not his stained fingers or his gray temples or the starched white shirt he always wore. Instead, I searched the pines alone, my ears tuned for a mellifluous song. But the owls hooted, and the cart wheels rattled, and the good doctor hummed a tuneless shanty, while beyond our small lantern, the forest lay dark as the grave.

"Dr. Rathbone's asked me to marry him," I said, when Aunt Elinor accosted me upon my arrival home. Though it was the small hours of the morning, and I'd not yet had time to run a bath to clean the stench of plague from me, she insisted upon serving me tea with that expectant look on her face, as she had every night since I started as a doctor's apprentice.

"Bless, I knew he would. Oh, Cat, didn't I tell you?"

She swooped in for a hug, daring to look offended when I held up a hand and said, "Please let me bathe."

But she followed me to the well, then to the fire, then to the tub, where the water rapidly cooled as she interrogated me. I placed a screen between us while I stripped down, setting my clothing aside to boil clean in lye later. In the decade since my mother's death, since I'd come to stay with her sister, I'd become adept at answering Aunt Elinor without truly devoting my full attention to her. And yet the line of questioning tonight was impossible to ignore.

After a dozen questions about rings and wedding gowns and dowries, after I'd finished wringing out the rope of my unruly chestnut hair, she grew unnaturally quiet. My blood chilled. Through the screen came Aunt Elinor's hesitant voice. "But, you did say yes, didn't you?"

I froze, the sponge hovering above my arm. "I said I'd consider it."

She groaned, a sound that held volumes and made her seem older than her forty years.

"I didn't reject him outright. I merely… asked for time." I sounded as tepid as the bathwater swirling around me, and I hated that.

"Cat," my aunt said, a gentle admonition.

"I heard your voice in my head, believe me. I know that twenty-five is bordering on unmarriageable, I know that I carry the burden of my mother's reputation, I know that Dr. Rathbone is my benefactor and I ought not to turn him down, but—"

"But have you considered that, even if you, a bastard daughter, had other marriage proposals, he'd be among the best? If others knew about your condition, they might be inclined to leave before the ceremony," she whispered the last part, not unkindly, as if it was some kind of scandal that I took to bed ill more days than not.

"Other suitors," my voice caught, "would never know. They'd leave the house for the day, and I'd stay home with my legs wrapped up and salve on my knuckles, if I were even allowed to practice my magic still."

I'd had other offers of marriage, of course. Ones that Aunt Elinor never knew about. They were bold declarations from lovers, mostly, whispered in a post-tryst haze, and to each one, I doled out a firm rejection. I saw my would-be fiancés around town still. Daniel MacLear, apprenticing under the local blacksmith. Ciaran Billingsley, still a stablehand, the same place I'd tussled with him in the hay. Liam O'Hara, working a plot of his own land now. Each took extra care with my aching joints as we lay together, and each watched me guzzle a contraceptive brew to keep from following my mother into ignominy. Each married another woman within a year of their failed proposals.

The problem was not suitors learning of my illness or reputation. It was that I had no desire to marry and even less desire to marry the good doctor Rathbone, a man so old that he could pose as the father I'd never met.

"You value your independence, I know this. But marriage is not the death of freedom," my aunt said with a sigh, her silhouette shifting beyond the screen. "In a decade or two, or sooner, you'll be widowed, and then no one will ever care a whit for what you do."

"You speak from experience," I said. Aunt Elinor had been widowed a year after her wedding, inherited her late husband's property, and brought in a paltry income from her apothecary's potions, now greatly supplemented by my work as a healer.

"I do. But who knows? You might even be happy before then."

"Perhaps," I conceded.

But as I lay in bed that night, my window cracked open and curtains fluttering in the delicate breeze, the haunting memory of a banshee's hymn rang in my ears, and it made even the ache in my knees not burn so badly. And I knew then that I would never again feel as I did when I locked eyes with her in the woods, not with anyone else, and that I would never be satisfied with anything less.

Our first meeting was not, blessedly, our last. Or, perhaps, not blessedly, for each night I saw her began with an urgent knock upon my door—

Dr. Rathbone, the customary birdlike plague mask clutched in one hand and a sachet of pressed flowers in the other—and ended with a red cross upon another's, a quarantine order spoken through windows to its inhabitants.

If not for her, I might have protested: plague moved quickly from fever and chills to gangrene, and by the time most sought our services, they were too far gone for Dr. Rathbone to even waste time with the leeches, let alone send me in. But he realized after our first night that there was great value in checking the other inhabitants of a quarantined house for early signs and offering my healing services before they, too, followed their relatives into an unmarked grave—for a hefty price, naturally.

Each night, I stumbled back to our carriage, my legs already stiffening, my anguish made bearable only by the wordless song echoing through the hills and the fleeting glimpses of pure white dancing between the trees. What little I saw sustained me through the long drive back, as the soulless eyeholes of Dr. Rathbone's discarded mask bored into me, and the man himself eyed me with barely disguised hunger, waiting, I knew, for an answer. But for four days, I left him sorely disappointed, for I was gone with pain by the time he dropped me at my door. How grateful I was for that, and for the hot baths I'd draw afterwards. For Aunt Elinor's tea, served with an expectation that I now found the strength to dodge.

But I could not escape forever. On the fifth day, after we pulled sheets over a young couple—first, the husband, then hours later, the wife—he stopped me on my way out the door. His mask still on and voice muffled, he asked me, "Have you considered?"

I might have played coy, but in that moment, it was all I could do not to laugh. The irony of my life. The woman who surely owned my heart was singing just outside the oilcloth window, and here I was, getting propositioned by a vulture.

"Did the couple remind you of us? Is that why you're asking?" I did not wait for his answer, but pushed past him into the night. "Because if so, I do not find a plague-wedding romantic or practical. It's tragic, truly."

As I lugged his bag into the carriage, I spotted my banshee drawing near, and my heart leapt. It was the only thing that kept me from shuddering in revulsion when Doctor Rathbone placed his hand upon my back. "What better time for us? You cannot catch the plague, but I do not know how long before I succumb."

Regrettably, there was nothing I could say to that. If I did not succumb when it swept through my village a decade ago, before the ache in my bones left me bedbound for weeks and I watched funerals from the window, then I would not succumb now, with every precaution.

"That is true," I said mildly, while my words drowned under banshee song. She was close enough now that I could see the color of her eyes, a strikingly clear blue against the paleness of her skin, and the wispy white lashes that adorned them. I wanted to smooth back the fine hairs that curled at her temples. I wanted to hear my name in her mouth, a bittersweet song, even knowing what that meant. I wanted to shake off the good doctor and instead sprint to her, to beg her to stay, to plead that her job and mine were two sides of the same coin.

I wanted, desperately and viciously.

"You don't sound convinced," Dr. Rathbone said. He moved past me, set his bag down, took up the reins.

"Great decisions are not generally made in less than a week's time, plague or no. Allow me some time to picture myself as a wife before I commit." My voice was more delicate than he or I expected, but then, these words were not intended for him. They were for the banshee, whose eyes never wavered from mine, even as Dr. Rathbone helped me onto the driver's seat after he mounted, then trapped my hand in his.

He had not yet removed his mask; the vulture Rathbone turned to me, with his soulless eyes and said, in his doctor voice, "You may not have the time you think, Catriona."

My banshee shrieked. The blood stilled in my veins. I pulled my hand from his abruptly.

"What do you mean?"

"Your aunt," he said simply. "Did you not notice how she rubbed her neck this evening? Or the extra layer of clothing she wore, and yet she still shivered? Or the sweaty sheen of her skin?"

"Her neck has troubled her for years, an ancient injury. And she's getting older. Perhaps it's just the end of her childbearing years coming sooner than usual. I've heard women afflicted with chills and sweats from that."

"Catriona."

Beside us, the banshee kept pace, the first time she had ever done so, and the fear began to set in. Those glimmers of song I heard ringing in my ears at night—were they more than just a phantom echo? Was she at my window, night after night, lying in wait for my aunt's soul? The good doctor sat calmly beside me as my voice rose. "You cannot possibly be right, because I took precautions. I never let her touch my clothing. I covered every windowsill with flowers to keep the miasma away. And I would've seen the signs before you."

"Would you have?" He asked. "I see the pain on your face even now. How likely is it that you've paid attention to another while in that haze?"

I did not answer him. I clutched my skirts tight in one hand and massaged my calves with the other, just to feel something outside of my own head, and to distract from the blur of white that raced barefoot beside us.

I was foolish. Weak. Pigheaded.

I was infatuated with a graveyard monster, a harbinger of doom whose connection felt divine only because she hungered for my familial blood, and though I seldom prayed, I did just then.

I kept my eyes fixed straight ahead as we neared my home. As usual, Doctor Rathbone helped me down, because I think my pain after these housecalls made him feel guilty. But it was not the good doctor this time, gray eyed and feigning chivalry. It was vulture-Rathbone, his bag already in hand, tugging me along behind him as my banshee glided closer.

I narrowed my eyes, my heart pounding a frantic song. "Leave us," I whispered under my breath. Her pale eyes widened in response, hand pressed against her lace-clad chest as if I'd dealt a fatal blow. She stopped her song then, as Doctor Rathbone flung open my door to the shabby interior, as dark as a grave.

"I'll get us some light and bar the shutters while you go find my aunt," I said, swiftly shutting the door behind us, all traces of white blessedly vanishing. I could handle no distractions, and I hoped the quiet meant my message had been received. That I had some power in me beyond servitude, after all.

I busied myself fumbling with flint at the hearth, then dipping as many sticks of tallow into the flame as I could. My hands shook, dreadfully, as I carried them towards the low voice of Dr. Rathbone in Aunt Elinor's bedroom.

The shutters rattled against my banshee's shriek—not dispelled after all—while the doctor beckoned me closer. A matted expanse of dark hair clung to my aunt's head and neck, a swollen lymph node nestled like an egg beneath it. Her limp hand dangled, blackened fingers nearly brushing a half-filled bowl of blood and bile.

I feared the worst until I saw the shallow rise of her chest beneath layers of bedding. "We don't have much time," Doctor Rathbone said. "If you'll grab the leeches for me, they may drain the pestilence from her before—"

"No."

"Catriona, it is the best way to ensure she'll live."

A glimmer of song flitted into my mind just then, an irrational urge that settled into my bones with such conviction, it almost felt divine.

I shook my head. "She doesn't take well to bloodletting. Please, I can handle this." His mask revealed nothing of his emotions, and yet I felt the questioning gaze. His hand reached for the jar, and I darted forward to grab his wrist.

"If we're to be married, I'd like to know that my husband will trust my judgment in family matters," I said. He paused to consider. My banshee wailed again, and my heart raced terribly, before he gave a small nod.

"Very well. I suppose you'd want me to mix something for your pain when you're done?"

I was so lightheaded with relief that I almost forgot to answer. But then, once I heard his heavy footsteps echoing down the hall, I came back to myself so fast, I could hardly breathe. A fire filled my veins. I forgot my pain; I knew what I had to do.

Driven by a mournful call, I took my aunt's damp fingers in my own and I closed my eyes. Her soul was still strong, but darkened by sickness. I reached into the shining light of mine, feeling it mingle alongside the edges of hers. And I gave, and I gave, and I gave.

Five days, I lingered in a laudanum-induced stupor, voices weaving around me, dreamlike. Mostly Rathbone in those first few days, come to administer another dosage whenever I wrenched awake, hot with pain. I might have asked about Aunt Elinor, because I felt a hand on my brow once, a reassurance in my ear, "She will live, Catriona. I will put the leeches on her tonight to draw out the rest of the sickness." The delirium took me before I could find the strength to protest.

Later, towards the end of my illness, I cracked my eyelids open to catch a glimpse of my aunt, stroking my damp hair back. "I cannot thank you enough," she said, and I smiled through the ache in me. "It was a godsend, what you and Doctor Rathbone did. He is a good man, Catriona. You'll do well to marry him."

I pretended I did not hear that part, that it was drowned out by the constant echo of banshee song. Because it was. If Rathbone was steadfast with medicine, my banshee was vigilant in song. I heard her constantly, though strongest when he came by—or perhaps, that was just when my senses were most acute—and it tumbled my thoughts together. She did not come for my aunt, else she would have left; I had banished the last dregs of plague from Aunt Elinor before I collapsed, and I knew that it would never strike her twice. And I knew she did not come for me, because my pain was not lethal, though it often felt so.

I became convinced, perhaps irrationally, that it was Rathbone she sought, and I resented every drop of laudanum that passed my lips. If I could just leave my bed, even if I needed a cane to do it, I would confront her and end this useless dance forevermore. I could not decide whether she haunted me or saved me, whether I longed to throw open the shutters to her white light or seal her out.

But on the sixth day, when Rathbone declared that he would no longer waste his medicine supply on me, that my pain should be bearable by now, I resolved to find my answer. He had not yet left, but was in another room saying his farewells to my aunt; his footsteps crossed to the door thrice, and each time she pulled him back with an offer of tea. The final time, he accepted. The warm chamomile scent drifted to me, their chatter hovering around the edges of my hearing. I rose on aching knees, fumbling at the latch to my shutters, before a sudden wind drew them open.

But it was no nightly breeze. There she stood, my banshee, her pale hands pressed against the sill. In the moonlight, her hair shone silver. I had never wanted her more than I did then.

"You weren't here for my aunt. I feared you were. But that was you, who whispered in my ear that I could save her, wasn't it?" My voice trembled, but I took strength in my banshee's confident nod.

"It was not her time." When she spoke, it was still a song, melodious and lilting. Like nothing I'd ever heard before. "Not yet. I could not see her die when there are still years beyond her."

"Thank you for that. But please answer me this. When I saw you first, during the house calls, you weren't there for them, either, were you? Though it was their time?"

"I was not."

"So only he and I are the common threads here, and my pain cannot kill me. You linger here for him."

"That I cannot say. The ancient laws prohibit me from telling an omen of death to the living." The corner of her full lips quirked up mischievously, and I understood then: it was a game.

"We all land in the grave eventually. You know that better than most, I feel. Can you at least tell me how soon I might expect his end? Or what he might die of? I suppose it'll be plague," I added, trying to read any clues in her expressive face.

Her blue eyes twinkled, like a river in early dawn. "I've never heard someone so fervently wish for their betrothed's death."

"Then you have not spent much time in the company of young women. We all wish it, I'm certain, especially if the intended's as old and patronizing as mine." I reached my hand out to hers, and she did not pull away. "Besides, he is not my betrothed yet. Your answer will fully decide me, either way."

She tilted her head. Her hand beneath mine was cold, her fingers delicate. Her other hand ghosted along my jawline, sending pleasurable shivers down my spine. "You give me too much power, Catriona."

"Only the amount you deserve…"

"Moira."

"Moira." Her name felt like a first kiss, delicate and saccharine. "If I hadn't seen you that first night, I might've found myself at the altar already. There's a sort of power in knowing that I've held off on marriage for a reason, because I refuse to settle for less than what I have here."

"Which is?"

"You."

Said out loud, it was terrifying. With my past loves, I'd let myself be chased, knowing that they would always fall deeper than I did, that they would be no more than a pleasant distraction from my night shifts and my pain. But this, this was my heart at stake. My eyes never wavered from hers as the words tumbled into the clear midnight air. As first shock, then desire, crossed her face, and her eyes dipped down to my lips.

"If I kiss you, promise me you won't take this as an answer," she said hesitantly, her thumbnail brushing my lower lip. "I have no power over the living. Just a desire for a healer who knows her own worth and is close to divine. It's lonely in the woods, Catriona, and you're the only one who sees me as I am."

I pressed myself up and out of the first-floor window, ignoring the screaming ache in my knees. My fingers slipped through the white waves of her hair, my lips breathless inches from hers. "I will promise you my very soul if I can call you mine."

She inhaled deeply, her delicate white lashes fluttering shut. I closed my eyes, the blinding white of her an imprint on the underside of my lids. I leaned in closer, her forest-scent all around me, and then—

"Catriona, you'll catch your death."

I pulled myself from the window so abruptly that black spots danced in my vision and I landed painfully on my side. When I glanced over at the doorway, there Aunt Elinor and Rathbone stood, her hand on his elbow.

"Perhaps she could do with a bit less laudanum," she tiptoed up to whisper in his ear. "I think she's hallucinating again."

"I've not given her any. Catriona, whatever madness has gotten into you, please see fit to return to yourself before tomorrow night's rounds. And certainly before we're to be wed." He turned now to me, shaking off my aunt and moving to close the shutters. I stretched up a hand to slap him away; a flash of naked hatred crossed his features.

"I am hot with pain. I sought a nightly breeze."

"You were talking to yourself."

"Since my own aunt came so close to death, I decided I'd say my prayers to the families of the dearly departed. I hadn't thought to do so before this, but I want to make a habit of it."

He raised an eyebrow, before his expression settled into some disappointed sigh. "Well, if you must do that, don't do it in my presence. I will pick you up at seven sharp tomorrow night."

"I will see you then," I said, and I inhaled deeply once I heard the door shut behind him. I waited for Aunt Elinor, too, to say her goodnights. Then, my heart pounding painfully, I fixed my eyes on the shutters once more, praying that Moira had stayed or that she'd return again.

But the night sky was as clear and dark as ever, bereft even of stars, and no voice echoed through my dreams.

True to form, Rathbone arrived the following night as he did every other, mask beside him and cart wheels rattling down the cobblestone path. My joints were still aching, my limbs sluggish and head heavy, but I knew that if I tried to protest, he would drag me along anyway. He always felt my pain was an exaggeration, but would dose himself with laudanum at the slightest stiffness in his fingers.

As I pulled myself up beside him, I tried to remind myself that his arrival was secretly a blessing. After all, enduring his company meant the promise of Moira. But at that moment, I did not feel blessed.

"We have three calls tonight," he said, his voice drowned beneath the crack of the reins and the clomping of hooves. "I've lost business during the week I was caring for you."

"Plague?" I asked.

He scoffed. "What else? I'll still need you, though. They're large families, half the members afflicted and half not, so you'll check them for signs while I tend to the sick. Heal any and all. I'll be charging double."

I pressed my lips into a thin line. What could I say to that, when I'd be defying him later to pray at the altar of Moira's touch?

We drove onward in silence to the first cottage, home to the healthy couple who'd knocked on Rathbone's practice that morning and their three fevered children. I stood by the oilcloth window, my eyes trained on Rathbone and his leeches as always, but my ears attuned to the potential of Moira's song. I tried not to let my disappointment show when the night was quiet, when vulture-Rathbone cleared his throat beneath that dreadful mask and said, "Catriona, have you forgotten your duties? None are too far gone."

I scrubbed a hand between my brows, hoping to smooth out the budding ache there. I should have known this was coming, that he'd see how I healed Aunt Elinor and know I had this hidden power in me. But I did my duty. I stepped forward, taking the leech jar from him and nestling it back into its bag. I placed my hands onto sweat-slick foreheads and pulled from some deep well within me, thinking only of Moira to distract from the exhaustion.

I pretended I could hear her. But perhaps it was only a figment of my imagination, because when we finally stepped outside, Rathbone's pockets bulging with coins, the woods were dark as ever, lit only by our single lantern.

"You did well," he said, and I both glowed and seethed with rage. It had been so long, three whole years, since I'd heard a scrap of praise from him. But his praise was my pain, and he did not even care.

We drove on to another house, another agony for me. Another silent, dim night. I counted down the hours. I massaged my aching calves when I thought no one was looking. I slammed open shutters, claiming that I needed to clear the air of miasma, and I blinked back tears.

Perhaps he'd scared her away, or perhaps whatever sickness that plagued him had miraculously healed itself, and I'd never see Moira again. Either way, I knew my answer to his proposal, should he mention it again. I had seen another way; I had tasted freedom, and it tasted like the sweet bloom of a riverbed. I could not shackle myself to him now, even if he only lived a day beyond our wedding night.

We'd nearly reached the last housecall before disaster struck. This one was as remote as our first plague call had been, up the side of a Highland hill, the dirt road studded with rocks. Our horse protested and bucked against the turning carriage. I thought I'd be sick, both from pain and from motion. Beside me, Rathbone cursed. I held on tightly as we swayed, drawing nearer and nearer to the edge, as I closed my eyes against the sight, and then he grabbed my arm. With one hand, he tugged back the reins so our horse reared up and I heard a sudden crack. I tumbled into him. He nearly slid off the side.

When he pulled me out, as I clung to his clothing like some disgusting, lovestruck damsel, I gasped at the damage. The axle of our carriage was cracked, our horse looking wild and caged as he untangled her from the wreck.

"I don't think we'll be making that final call," I said, my voice echoing among the rocks.

"A keen observation, Catriona." He sighed, dusting his hands off on his oddly pristine trousers. "I don't suppose you could walk back to town?"

"If you hadn't made me heal even the plague-afflicted while I was still recovering from the last use of my magic, perhaps." I could not keep the edge from my voice.

"Can you at least stay here while I find shelter, then?"

"I can," I said, as I watched his retreating back.

He returned quickly, much to my dismay, claiming to have found an abandoned cottage along the hills. His mask was off, clutched in his hand, and I noticed a faint sheen along his brow. He was shivering, though the autumn air was mild.

"The walk was too much for you?" I asked, and his eyes raked over me in confusion.

"I haven't the faintest idea what you're talking about," he said as we approached our nightly dwelling. The door was already propped open, the hearth lit, branches now burning within its depths. Two wicker chairs had been dragged before it and into one of these, Rathbone folded himself, wrapping his doctor's coat around him like a shawl.

I took the other, the closest to the window, and it was then, in the shadow of the fire, that I saw it. A blackish swelling, just below his jaw. As if on cue, a brilliant white light beyond the thin windows. A melodious voice.

But then my heart sank. For if his death was imminent, then how could I convince Moira to stay beyond that? Was I to surround myself with the dying forevermore, so I might catch a glimpse of her in the night?

I shook my head to clear such thoughts as Rathbone said, suddenly, "I suppose your aunt would find this improper, us staying the night together, unwed."

"Unless you can find a priest at this hour and a chapel, unwed we'll stay. Also, I do not intend to share a bed with you, regardless of marital status."

"Because you are so chaste? I know of your lovers, Catriona."

"Because I ache, dreadfully, in no short part due to your greed. And that is why I'll never be yours." Despite my pain, I stood up abruptly and crossed the few steps to the window. I could not bear the thin, oily sound of his voice any longer.

In the corner of my eye, I saw him move, too. Saw him withdraw something glinting and silver from his pocket. I threw open the shutters to Moira, her eyes flicking first to him, then to me. And when I spun around, I knew. Truly knew.

"I tire of these games," said Rathbone, swaying towards me with a scalpel in his hand and a fever in his eyes. "Like a child, you string me along and placate me. But you owe me. I gave you a job when no one else would have you. I lost five days' income to care for your pitiful illness. Tell me, do you really prefer the grave to a life with me?"

I felt the press of Moira's ghostly hand along my collarbone, her voice whispering promises of the great beyond in my ears. I raised my eyes to meet his. I ignored the pounding of my heart.

"Yes," I said simply.

When he advanced towards me, backing me against the sill like some animal, I wrapped my leg around him to draw him in, and I watched his eyes widen. His knife sunk into my heart with surgical precision, my blood spattering crimson upon him, my head swimming.

I would not have greeted death half so easily if I'd known that it would hurt worse than any ache I'd ever felt. But when I turned my head to meet Moira's eyes, her lips pressed against mine and my blood sang in my veins. She cupped my jaw with spectral hands, pulling me closer and closer, out into the hills. In the window, a dreadful tableau played out: Rathbone splayed across the bleeding husk of me, both of us sinking down to the filthy floor.

In a few hours, his fingers would blacken with gangrene and his lymph nodes would swell. He'd stink dreadfully, if he was ever found, or he'd be a meal for some hillside beast. Where his soul would go, I did not know, and I did not care.

But I would never die, for didn't you know the other half of the legend? A banshee is the soul of a murdered woman, transformed to a righteous creature beyond the grave.

Breathless, Moira and I sprinted up the hills, our hands intertwined, my legs stronger than I could have ever imagined.

"When I saw you that first night, did you always know?" I asked. As we scaled the highest peak, the night spread out before us like a map of possibilities.

She turned to me, her eyes moonlit. "That you were destined to join me in eternity? Of course not. I came for the doctor's soul, and I'll take it in a day's time. But now that you're here, will you be mine?"

"You already know I'll say yes," I whispered, breathless before another for the first time in my life.

"Well then," she said, voice full of mischief. "Shall we wait for his end?"

I shook my head. "No, I've had enough of the wills of men. Show me your world, Moira."

Then she did, from the farthest reaches of the Highlands to the graveyard we call ours, where we rest each morning, curled up together, and wait to haunt the night with glorious song.

LADY OF THE DARK
TAYLOR HUBBARD

Ghizol was always fresh and clean.

It was nothing like Ascal imagined only a few years ago. She grew up hearing stories of the orc settlement of Ghizol being a place that produced war and nothing else. The elves of the Kingdom of Athowen, her homeland, cared little for accuracy, she came to discover. All it took was actually seeing Ghizol to understand its beauty.

Greeted by clear skies and bright sunshine with pleasant heat permeating the wild grasses, Ascal took a long inhale of the sweet aroma. After her journey through dense woodland, the valley Ghizol was settled in was a welcome sight. There were only so many leaves and bark to look at before boredom gnawed at her when she was barely halfway through her trip.

Her horse followed the familiar path to the stables, ready to receive the treats the stable boy spoiled her with. Normally she might argue, but figured there was no harm in her horse eating a few extra crabapples after the long journey from Athowen.

Maybe it was because she was in a better mood whenever she came to Ghizol.

When Ascal slipped off her steed in front of the stable, Gurak, an orc who only just reached his adulthood greeted her as he took her reins. He had grown to be a few inches taller than Ascal since her last visit. He was truly blessed by his growth spurts. His tusks barely protruded from his lower lip, but the wider his smile, the more tusk was visible, reaching his upper lip.

"Morning! You're early," he said, immediately offering up a piece of carrot to the horse who greedily snatched it up with a satisfied whinny. "The trip went well?"

"Good morning to you," Ascal said, stepping away to give the boy room to work. "I made better time than usual today. It was an easy ride this time. No raiders."

Gurak snorted as he stroked the mare's mane. "The raiders in the area must know your schedule. They're not interested in getting their asses kicked anymore."

"Well, perhaps your chief should be thanking me for keeping raiders away with my mere presence." Ascal grinned when Gurak let out a full belly laugh. "I won't complain about an easy trek, though."

Though truth be told, she had a hard time sleeping the day before.

More and more often, the promise of Ghizol set her nerves alight with a pleasant buzz. Something she wasn't used to back in Athowen. She could understand why Silvyr, once under her protection in Athowen, chose to remain here with the chief who stole him over a year ago. He fit in perfectly with the orcs of Ghizol, finding his place at the chief's side as though he had always been there. Ascal's welfare visits, a duty she put upon herself to protect her once prince, were no longer necessary. And yet . . .

"There you are," Salthu's voice, deep and firm, rang out in the morning air and Ascal's lips tugged into a smile.

And yet there was Salthu.

"Here I am." Ascal approached the powerful woman, who stood more than a head taller than herself. All hard lines and thick muscle, viridian skin adorned with scars of marvelous suede, Salthu was a force of nature in her own right. Her hair was black as raven feathers, her eyes like fresh daffodils, and when she smiled, her silver-capped tusks pressed into her upper lip. "You came prepared."

Salthu wore her sparring leathers, much like Ascal wore her own, despite the early hour and peaceful morning. The routine was comforting and natural. Ascal would check on Silvyr, spar with Salthu, and return to Athowen. As infrequent as her journeys to Ghizol were, every time she left, she wanted to return right away. She found herself making more excuses to return to Ghizol.

"Well, I figured you'd want to fight after I broke the news to you," Salthu said, immediately raising her hands when Ascal's face fell. "Everything's fine! But Silvyr isn't here."

Ascal's eyes narrowed on Salthu. "*What?*"

"Listen, spitfire." Salthu snorted, shaking her head and holding up her hands as though she were the guilty party. "Brokil left on business, and Silvyr, the little shit that he is, snuck off with him."

That did *not* soothe Ascal's worries at all. "Who let him go off? What business is Brokil on? Doesn't he know that Silvyr cannot fight? *At all?*" Ascal sputtered, pure disbelief at Silvyr's idiocy. Once they returned to Ghizol, Ascal would let Silvyr have a piece of her mind.

"He's with the chief, and he'll be safe with him." Salthu's lips curled, trying to contain a laugh. If she thought to console Ascal's racing heart, she failed. "If he's safe anywhere, it's next to Brokil. That man would sooner die than let anything happen to Silvyr. Besides, it's a diplomatic meeting. Brokil is just finalizing ore trade contracts."

Even Ascal couldn't argue that Silvyr was just as safe with Brokil as he was here and forced herself to take a breath. Overreacting would do nothing to make Silvyr return to Ghizol right that second anyhow.

"I suppose you're right. Still, he's an idiot for leaving," she said, forcing her words to come out slow and concise as she crossed her arms over her chest.

"Oh, I'm not arguing that," Salthu agreed as she reached out to place her hand on Ascal's shoulder. The weight was comfortable and brought more relief than Ascal expected. "Come to the training grounds with me. You're tense and you need to unwind."

Fighting back the smile that pulled at the corners of her lips, Ascal followed Salthu's lead to the training grounds. It was still early enough that no one else had secured a spot to spar in, giving the two of them first pick. Not that they needed it. They always chose the same area to fight.

Hard packed dirt and free of foliage or cover of any kind, it was the perfect place for the orcs of Ghizol to train. It immediately put Ascal at a disadvantage being outside of her realm of experience and training. A challenge she enjoyed every time she came.

Once they stepped in the arena, it was like no time had passed since the last visit as they fell into their routine. They launched toward each other, daggers clashing in the morning sun. They went through the motions, slow at first. Circling. Analyzing.

Ascal felt alive again inside Salthu's powerful gaze.

The first few times they'd fought, Salthu threw Ascal to the ground with such ease that she couldn't tell if her heart raced in anger or admiration.

They were damn near evenly matched, but Salthu knew how to fight directly. How to catch an attack coming from straight ahead. How to parry and counter and use trickery to turn the tides of battle in her favor. Unlike Ascal, who fought in the shadows, Salthu thrived in the sunlight.

Ascal threw herself at Salthu, raising her blades to bring them down in a high arc. The moment the corner of Salthu's lips twitched, Ascal knew she made a mistake. Salthu ducked down and shoved her elbow into Ascal's stomach, knocking her to the ground, punching out the remaining air in her lungs.

"My win," Salthu grinned, the silver capped tusks pressing into her upper lip, leaving behind gentle dimples.

"You fight dirty," Ascal wheezed, rolling onto her hands and knees.

"You fight too clean," Salthu countered with a low laugh, setting her hand on Ascal's back to steady her. "Sometimes that knight's honor bullshit just gets in the way."

"It works better when there's more than one of us," Ascal admitted with a laugh of her own. "Why don't we try fighting in the forest? I bet you'll be less smug then."

"I don't think so," Salthu stood, offering her hand to lift Ascal to her feet. "Besides, I like seeing your face every time you lose. You have a cute little pout. It's *very* knightly."

Ascal's cheeks flared with heat that continued to rise to the tips of her elongated ears and she opened her mouth to chastise Salthu for her ridiculous 'observation.' The words fell away when a sudden clamoring to their side drew their attention.

Frantic and disheveled, a woman stumbled over her feet toward them, covered in soil and hair clinging to her tear-stained cheeks. Without thinking, Ascal dashed to meet her with Salthu at her side.

"Maka," Salthu grunted when the woman collided with her. She put her hands on the woman's shoulders, steadying her on her feet. "Maka, what's the matter?"

"My-my." Maka struggled to speak through the tears streaming down her face. She grabbed at Salthu's wrists, digging trenches in the skin with her nails as she choked on another sob.

Gentle, but with a firmness that made Ascal's heart stutter, Salthu shook Maka's shoulders once. "Speak, Maka. Tell me what happened? Are you hurt?"

"No!" Maka took a long, shuddering breath. "My girl. She was taken. *Something* took her from the farm. It was like a shadow and it ripped her out of our garden. It *took* her!"

Ascal locked eyes with Salthu for only a moment.

"Show me where," Salthu demanded when she brought her attention back to Maka. "Sorry Ascal. I'm cutting our visit short."

"I'm coming with you," Ascal said, slipping her daggers into the sheaths. Turning to Maka, Ascal tried to offer a reassuring smile. "Let's go. There's no time to waste."

Thankfully, Salthu didn't argue with her. She knew that Ascal wouldn't budge on something like this, nor would she get in the way. It was bold of her to even suggest that Ascal would simply walk away after learning that a child had been taken by something clearly nefarious. It went directly against her oath to protect the meek. Her '*Knight's Honor Bullshit*' simply wouldn't allow it.

Walking through Ghizol, Ascal followed Salthu and the harried Maka up toward the farmland until the scent of manure and fresh greenery and produce hit her like a wave. The blending of two opposite sensations rattled her. Athowen didn't have farmland like this and it was a shock every time Ascal came this way, no matter how she tried to brace herself.

Maka's home wasn't too far from the edges of Ghizol proper. Far enough away for her to have a large parcel of land for her crops and livestock. It was a simple wooden home with a fenced in garden in the back. Wide open with many avenues of attack and escape. They didn't linger when Maka opened the gate to her garden, letting them inside to examine the scene.

"Uthra was pulling weeds so we could sow our seeds when the thing took her. It was like a dog, but so black I couldn't see fur." Maka sniffled as she brought them to an upturned basket. "It didn't make noise either. I only heard Uthra screaming for me."

As she spoke, Maka's words morphed into a pitiful sob.

Careful not to disturb too much of the garden, Ascal gingerly stepped through the dirt. The soil around the basket held the markers of a struggle. Little feet dug their heels into the ground, kicking and thrashing against whatever grabbed her. Tough fingers shoved into the dirt, pulling clumps out of the earth. The marks continued through the garden until they reached the fence and picked up again outside the wooden structure.

Uthra was a fighter, there was no doubt about that.

"The trail is heading toward the forest," Salthu told Ascal under her breath.

"It appears so," Ascal agreed, taking a long inhale to calm herself. "Are you a decent tracker?"

"Decent enough. We don't have time to find another one anyways." Salthu stepped out of the garden and turned her head toward Maka. "We're going after her. You stay here. If you follow us, you may make it worse."

"But that's *my* daughter." Maka stepped forward to argue the point.

If there was one thing Ascal knew about the orcs of Ghizol, it was that they trusted their leaders to protect them with everything they had. Clearly, Salthu took her position as interim chief seriously while Brokil was away, and she pushed her shoulders back and tilted her chin up.

"Maka," Salthu started. "Stay here. I need you here in case Uthra returns on her own. Ascal and I can handle whatever took her. I won't argue this point and risk Uthra's safety *and* yours."

Maka's lips tightened and Ascal worried her tusks may pierce her lip from the pressure. After a moment of bouncing her eyes between Salthu and Ascal, Maka finally took a step back.

"I'll be here," Maka reluctantly agreed.

With the matter settled, they left the farm and headed for the forest. Ascal tried to imagine what took Uthra. What Maka was describing. What kind of beast would be made of shadows? How could a shadow grab something let alone a *child*? There was nothing in any of her studies, limited as they were, that pointed to the creature Maka described. It sounded mythical.

"What do you think took the girl?" Ascal asked once they were far enough away from Maka's farm. Salthu's brows pinched tight together.

"I don't know. I've never heard of something like that," Salthu said, curling her hands into tight fists until her knuckles paled. "Dogs made of shadows? Is such a thing possible?"

"Sounds like a black dog to me." It was the only thing that made sense. "Maybe a wolf?"

"Wolves aren't common in the area. They've learned to stay away from our farms," Salthu was quick to respond. "But it makes the most sense. Perhaps it's rabid or starved and confused?"

"Let's hope it's too confused to hurt Uthra," Ascal said, more to herself than Salthu, but the woman nodded nonetheless.

The farmland sprawled into meadow and the forest beckoned them closer. The unnatural line separating the meadow from the treeline spoke of the industrialization Ghizol brought to the area. Though the care to keep the forest mostly intact wasn't lost on Ascal.

She expected birdsong as they approached. Or the rustling of leaves from the fauna within. But only silence enveloped the darkness within the trees. For the first time, Ascal's stomach curled into a tight knot when she stepped beyond the threshold. Salthu was equally quiet, she wondered if the other woman experienced the same sensation in her belly.

If she did, she hid it perfectly.

Silence in the forest could only mean one thing and Ascal was prepared to face whatever it was that dwelled within. Usually *Ascal* was the one bringing the forest to its knees, forcing it into submission when she slunk through the underbrush. A predator herself.

Pulling a dagger with one hand, and her short sword with the other, Ascal rolled her fingers over the hilt, using their familiarity to calm her racing heart. Hardened and experienced she may be, the thrill of the hunt and the promise of a fight, a *real* fight, never failed to send fire through her veins.

"You lead, I'll follow." Ascal lifted herself to her toes to breathe into Salthu's ear.

She didn't wait for Salthu to finish nodding. She slipped into the brush, blending with the flora around her. She learned long ago how to move without thought in the forest. How to become one with the leaves, immaterial like the air that settled in the greenery.

To become a shadow herself.

Shrouded in eerie gloom, Ascal stalked the orc woman leading the way, pausing only to examine the forest floor. Trampled leaves and ruined soil guided their path. Salthu knelt over the same markings, running thick fingers within shallow divots in the dirt. Ascal remained concealed, letting Salthu continue her work while she flicked her eyes across the woodland. Her heart thundered and she pushed herself to another vantage point, unheard and unfound by anything around them.

Besides the scuffs in the ground, there was no sign of the girl or the creature that took her. Ascal's stomach churned. Shouldn't she hear *something*? Crying or growling or some sort of noise within the silence around them?

Brilliant amber drew her attention back to Salthu, her eyes shining in the bleakness as they darted all around. Salthu's failure to find Ascal left her with a gentle grin on her lips before she returned her attention ahead of herself. Ascal's grip on her weapons tightened as she followed, ignoring the growing heat in her face.

An unnatural darkness descended the further they ventured into the forest, the silence also carrying an abnormal weight. It settled on Ascal's shoulders like a leaden veil, pressing her down and slowing her gait. Glancing at Salthu, she wondered if that same pressure pushed against Salthu. If she noticed how *sinister* the stench of the dark was. If dread was pooling in her stomach. The same dread that settled in Ascal's, pulling her back to her first campaign when she was fresh and new and had no clue what she would be facing.

She eyed Salthu again. Eyed the tense curve of her muscles in the shadows of the surrounding leaves. Eyed her as she hesitated. A movement so slight that Ascal would have missed it if she wasn't so focused on the orc.

Bending low to the ground, Salthu shifted beneath the brush as she moved forward. Following her eye line, Ascal caught what had the warrior kneeling, her own mouth dropping slightly.

How did she miss it?

The girl, curled up with her knees tucked tight to her chest and her face pressed to her knees, cowered in the presence of three wolves.

Not wolves.

Creatures.

Whatever they were, they didn't come from this world. They couldn't. There was nothing else made of darkness like these beasts. Ascal struggled to make out their features, darker than moonless night that billowed and snarled. Their limbs dripped and oozed, the blackness falling off of them dissipating into the air.

They padded around each other, their smoke swirling and caressing the tendrils as they passed their companions.

Then there were the eyes. Sharp and hollow, yet somehow bright with a sickening hue of corrupted sunlight. Even a glimpse sent rolling chills down Ascal's spine and she took a steadying breath.

Perhaps more alarming was how they left the girl alone. Those things had brought the girl into the forest, yet from Ascal's vantage, she wasn't injured. Terrified and helpless, yes, but unharmed. The creatures moved—*stalked*—like they were waiting for something.

Salthu raised her free hand, holding up two fingers and Ascal's nerves immediately settled to a gentle buzzing in her fingertips. *Routine.*

Salthu's signal was the only warning Ascal got before Salthu threw herself into the clearing with a furious battle cry that shattered the silence. The beasts snapped their heads to her, garish white fangs bared and dripping with inky muck.

Following her lead, Ascal shot through the trees, remaining hidden until she burst through the brush.

While the beasts smashed into Salthu, chomping down on her bracers and clawed into her leathers, Ascal flurried through the treeline toward the first beast. Her blades tore through its flesh with little resistance. Acrid smoke filled her lungs, burning the breath she took down to her core, and though it threatened to seize her insides, she let herself fall into muscle memory to follow through to disappear within the trees again.

The other two beasts didn't notice their fallen companion, and if they did, they didn't care. Their eyes didn't even flicker toward Ascal when she took down the first creature. They only continued to throw themselves at Salthu with wild abandon and no care for themselves or strategy, only snapping fangs against hardened metal.

Again, Ascal shot out of the treeline, slamming her dagger into the throat of the next beast, pulling the blade viciously through the sludgy flesh. Its cry rang through her ears and bile shot up her throat, spiraling into violent dizziness that she'd never felt before.

Disoriented, she tumbled back into the trees, her foot twisting awkwardly and she barely made it through when a snapping at her heel forced her into a rough stop. Serrated teeth sank into Ascal's ankle, and the pain that exploded up her calf and thigh sent her toppling to the ground.

"No you don't," Salthu's voice echoed behind her, followed by another anguished howl and the releasing of her ankle.

Turning back to the fray, Ascal caught the fleeting flicker of Salthu's blade coming down on the beast. Silence permeated the clearing and Ascal exhaled as she brought herself to her feet. Stepping toward Salthu, a sudden shock of pain burst up her leg and she stumbled out of the brush.

Strong arms grabbed her to keep her upright and Ascal let out a low groan. "My damn ankle," she muttered, putting weight on it again, only to grimace at the throbbing ache.

"Got ahead of yourself?" Salthu asked, the edge of teasing in her voice snapping Ascal's glare in her direction.

"That doesn't normally happen." Ascal grabbed Salthu's bracer to keep herself upright while she rolled her ankle. A definite sprain beneath the punctures. She couldn't tell what hurt more.

"It happens to the best of us. You know, one out of five—"

A sniffle in the quiet wood brought their attention back to the girl.

Ascal shoved aside the pain to reach her while Salthu easily passed Ascal's limping steps.

Dropping to her knees in front of the girl, Salthu cradled her face in large hands. The girl burst into tears the moment Salthu touched her, like her hands drew the noise directly from the child.

The girl, thank the gods, was mostly unharmed. She only had a single wound on her arm that bled through her pale blue linens. Salthu didn't hesitate to rip a portion of her own shirt into a long strip.

"Hey Uthra," Salthu said, her voice suddenly soft and sweet, twisting something in Ascal's chest, her heart fluttering. Carefully, she wrapped Uthra's arm and tied off the linen. It wasn't perfect by any means, but it would hold until they returned to Ghizol to bring her to a proper healer. "Ready to go home?"

Uthra nodded through her snot and tears, grabbing at Salthu's armor with such force that Ascal doubted they would be able to pry her off until they returned her to Maka. She couldn't blame the girl. Salthu was powerful and proven. Someone that the girl could rely on to ensure she made it home safely. Someone who didn't hesitate to do what needed to be done to protect her people. Even Ascal, proud and stoic as she liked to think she was, had to admit her admiration for the warrior.

Only when Uthra let out a sudden scream did Ascal realize that the rest of the forest was still unnaturally quiet. She spun around as a massive, clenched fist came down on them, covering the light that filtered through the leaves.

With no thought, Ascal threw herself to the side.

The ground beneath them shook violently when the fist collided, leaving a crater in its wake. When Ascal steadied herself back on her feet, she snapped her head to the other end of the clearing, relief blooming in her chest when she saw Salthu pull herself to her feet, the girl safe in her arms.

Ascal snapped her head back to the assailant, the size of the beast sending a shock of terror through Ascal's spine. How did none of them hear this thing coming?

Massive, standing far taller than either of them with a fist the height of Ascal herself, it pulled its lips back into a sinister snarl, blackened stringy mucus connecting its teeth. It stood on two long legs that rippled with taut muscle beneath the sludgy flesh, and turned its sunken jaundiced eyes on them through a barren curtain of greasy hair. Its protruding belly hung low beneath a concave chest with the same mucus in its mouth oozing down the length of its frame.

Putrid and decaying.

Had it not been so huge, Ascal would think it was a person once.

Ascal locked eyes with Salthu for only a moment, just long enough to see that Salthu had the same plan.

Then she launched herself back into the trees, ignoring the piercing flare in her ankle. When she caught sight of Salthu again, Uthra wasn't with her and she could only assume she was safe as Salthu swung her blade into the creature's leg, cutting through the papery flesh with a gruesome squelch.

Turning toward her, it released a harrowing howl into the forest. Ascal had to swallow the bile it brought up and force her head to stop spinning as the splitting sound tore through her, just like the sound the wolven shadows made. Pain radiated from the base of her skull as she pushed forward, blades in hand.

Flinging herself past the beast, she slashed and sliced at its chest. Putrid mucus wept from the wound and burned her nose and she forced herself to keep moving.

Its enormous fingers grasped her leg, snapping her to a sudden stop. In the same motion she was flung downward, crashing into the hard packed forest floor, punching out a heaving groan.

Agony followed an echoing *crack* that shot through her arm. Ascal clutched her blades tighter, bringing her arms up to slam the tips into the creature's wrist to free herself. Again it roared, grip tightening and digging curled claws into her calf, refusing to release its prey.

Cutting through the horrendous sound of the creature's shriek, Salthu's battlecry, long and loud, made the darkness quiver like sunlight parting the clouds. She brought her arms in a wide side arc to strike its thigh, but before she could make contact with the creature, it lifted Ascal off the ground again.

"Dammit, shit shit shit!" Ascal thrashed in its hold, trying without any success to pry the fingers off her leg. "*Fuck!*"

With a powerful swing, it slammed Ascal against Salthu's stomach, sending the both of them tumbling back.

Salthu hit the ground back first, skidding across the clearing while grabbing at Ascal to hold her steady. They both groaned, swiftly lifting their heads when they came to a stop.

"You alright?" Ascal asked, pulling herself upright, ignoring the new pain shooting up her arm.

"I'm fine." Salthu hurried to her feet, gripping her sword tight with one hand, pulling Ascal to her feet with the other. "You?"

"Good," Ascal lied with ease, adjusting her hold on her blades. Numbness coursed through her left hand, but as she turned back to the creature as it reared its head toward them, clomping to face them, Ascal grit her teeth and clenched her hands hard.

Sharp electricity blasted through her arm and Ascal swallowed a strangled cry as she dropped her second blade.

"Tch," Salthu huffed and Ascal didn't need to look at her to know she was rolling her eyes. "We can talk about your broken arm later."

Ascal didn't bother to examine the wound. She didn't need to. If she couldn't hold a blade, it was bad to put it mildly. Unfortunately they couldn't afford to linger on that. Not while this *thing* stared at them like they were a meal for the taking.

A broken arm was nothing if she was being eaten alive.

"Later," Ascal agreed, throwing herself at the beast. There was little she could do to fix her arm at that moment. Charging in was stupid and inadvisable at best, but she'd be damned if she sat back while Salthu fought on her own.

If she couldn't take it down, she could at least be a suitable distraction for Salthu.

As she collided with the beast, she shoved her blade into the meaty flesh of its thigh, slicing through cords of tendons and muscles. The beast roared and Ascal ignored the sickening sensation and flung herself backward right as a massive fist punched the ground where Ascal once stood. Another crater left behind in its wake.

She lost sight of her orc companion, but didn't linger too long on that. If Salthu was being smart, and there was little doubt that she was, then she was flanking the beast and using Ascal's distraction to her advantage.

Once more she attacked, bringing her blade in a side arc toward the beast's heel. All she needed to do was debilitate it. Stop it from moving. Stop it from *standing*. If she could do that, Salthu could make the final blow.

She just needed to reach it.

Her blade barely sliced into the creature's heel, drawing more of that sludgy blood before brutal talons slashed Ascal's side, sending her careening to the ground. Landing on her injured arm, she let out a strangled cry.

She barely recovered before the creature snatched her leg in a tight grip, claws impaling her thigh and she braced herself for another brutal assault. Lifted off the ground for only a moment, a wallowing shriek carried through the trees and hot mucus splattered across the forest floor in Salthu's wake. Her blade slashed across the creature's chest and Ascal hit the ground as she fell free of its hold and spiraled back, graceless and exhausted.

"Dammit." Ascal grunted and lifted herself upright, raising her blade to defend herself.

The beast threw its meaty fist down on her again and she lifted her arms in an 'X' over her head to catch the attack, bracing each muscle for impact even as fire flared through her wounds.

A shattering feral cry forced her hands loose, dropping her blade as it ricocheted through her system. Bursting from behind the creature, a warrior's cry that overshadowed the beast's on her lips, Salthu's blade sliced through its throat. Flesh tore and thick spurts of mucus sprayed across the forest floor.

Clawing at its own throat, the creature stumbled back. Its gurgled squalls echoed and were muted only by the thing crashing to its knees. The cry pittered out in wheezing breaths and the ground violently shook when it finally fell. Motionless. Dead.

Catching her breath, Ascal tried to pull herself to her feet. Every limb trembled and she almost lost the little footing she had until Salthu's powerful hand grabbed her uninjured arm, keeping her upright.

Though she didn't want to rely on anyone, Ascal let herself lean against Salthu.

She remained on guard, scanning the treeline for danger, refusing to be caught by surprise again. As Salthu sheathed her blade, birdsong began to filter through the leaves, signaling the returning peace to the forest.

"You're a fucking idiot," Salthu grumbled, her eyes darting all over her. "What the hell do they teach you in Athowen? Suicide missions?"

"Someone had to make sure you didn't get a cut on your pretty face," Ascal shot back, chuckling at the scowl on Salthu's lips.

"I'm serious. You're not leaving Ghizol for a while," Salthu told her. "And you're seeing a healer immediately."

Ascal put pressure on her ankle, wincing when her leg trembled with such ferocity that she feared it might give out. "Yeah maybe—"

"There is no 'maybe', you *are*."

Rolling her eyes, Ascal pulled her arm away from Salthu to sheath her own blades. She still hadn't looked at her arm, but in the calm of the clearing, the blood dripping beneath her bracers was sticky and suddenly too warm. She could feel the throbbing radiating from the middle of her forearm where it'd been snapped. Her fingers, though she was able to move them, were still tingling and numbness finally settled in after the high of battle.

She would deal with it later. That's what she did. Ignore pain and keep fighting.

"Where's the girl?" Ascal asked, scanning the foliage for the little orc child.

"H-here I am!" Uthra announced herself, crawling out from underneath the brush, her hair filled with twigs and leaves. Her wet cheeks were stained with dirt and she sniffled up running snot before she stood on wobbling knees.

After scrutinizing Ascal a final time, with a glare that clearly showed that she wasn't done scolding her yet, Salthu hurried over to Uthra and dropped hard to her knees before her. Uthra clutched at Salthu the moment she was within reach, her grip so tight Ascal wondered if the leathers would tear from her tiny strength. Salthu wrapped her arms around Uthra and lifted her to settle on her wide and muscular forearm.

In the daylight streaming through the treetops, breaking apart the oppressive darkness, Ascal took in the sight. Salthu was far better off than Ascal as far as injuries were concerned. Blood dripped down the side of her face from a gash across her forehead, but beyond a few forming bruises and scuffed armor, Salthu was relatively unhurt in comparison.

"Let's get you home," Salthu said, and the girl wiped her eyes, nodding.

The trip out of the forest was faster, though each step Ascal took spiked scalding flames up her leg. Salthu was right when she said Ascal wouldn't be leaving any time soon. Ascal was trained to ignore the pain, but the more they walked, the harder it was to ignore the extent of her injuries. Whatever that creature was, it fucked her up more than any opponent she'd faced before.

When they broke through the tree line, the fresh sunlight warmed her skin. Now out of the darkness of the forest, Ascal looked at her ruined arm. The stark white of bone jutted through the flesh and she let out a groan, more annoyed than pained. Salthu glanced at her for only a moment, but it was long enough for Ascal to see her rolling her eyes before she turned Uthra's head to keep her from seeing the worst of Ascal's wounds.

Uthra, exhausted from her ordeal, was all but mute the entire walk back to the farm. Save for the sniffles and soft hiccups, she might not have been there for all the noise she made.

The closer they got to the farm, the more Uthra's shoulders relaxed, and she lifted her head from Salthu's shoulder.

As her home came into view, the girl wriggled to get out of Salthu's grip, her smile bright enough to part rain clouds and her little tusks barely reaching past her upper lip. For a moment Ascal was reminded of a hyper kitten that didn't want to be held while it sped through a room. Salthu laughed and let the girl bounce out of her arms and bolt for home.

"Mama!" Uthra screamed.

In the garden, still pacing, Maka snapped her head toward them and all but catapulted over the fence to reach her little girl.

Scooping the child in her arms, Maka spun Uthra in a wide arc.

"Uthra! Oh thank the gods," she cried, kissing Uthra's face over and over and over again.

Ascal couldn't stop the smile from spreading while Salthu followed the child over. Ascal remained in place behind the fence, using the posts to hold herself up while she admired the three of them. Maka, with tears in her eyes, pulled Salthu into the hug while turning to Ascal to offer her a wide, tear-soaked smile.

It was sweet and Ascal returned the smile with a firm nod.

They spoke for only a few moments. Ascal didn't know exactly what was being said, but the 'thank yous' and 'how can I repay yous' were clear and quickly followed by Salthu shaking her head. As Ascal expected, Salthu wouldn't accept payment for what she did. Though, Ascal wouldn't either. Neither of them needed payment to do what they knew to be right.

"You," Salthu started after finally bidding Maka farewell. She stomped over with a tone that reminded Ascal of a drill sergeant and her back snapped straight immediately. "You are coming with me, and we're going to get Urzul to take a look at your arm and your foot. And your legs. And fucking hell, your ribs. Don't they teach you elves how to *not* get hit?"

Before Ascal could say anything or try to protest, Salthu scooped her up like a fresh bride, ignoring her indignant squawk at the manhandling. Heat flared in her cheeks and she would have smacked Salthu in the chest if her best smacking arm wasn't snapped.

"What the hell are you doing?" Ascal huffed, shifting in Salthu's arms.

"Stop moving. I'm getting you to stop putting weight on your ankle, you idiot," Salthu said, already walking toward Ghizol proper. "I should have carried you out of the forest too."

She carried Ascal with no effort, like she weighed nothing. Ascal had never felt so *small* before and the fact that it made her feel safe brought a new flush to her cheeks. She couldn't tell if she liked it or not, but she knew it felt warm.

"I can walk, you know," Ascal grumbled.

"No, you can't." Salthu laughed, bright and loud. "You're strong, but you're a bit dense, spitfire. When you get to Athowen, let them know your new title is 'Ascal the Dense Idiot.'"

Ascal scoffed, though a smile tugged at her lips regardless. "Better than my old title. I'd be able to use that one at least."

"What was your title before?"

"The Shadow's Gentleman." The words came out easier than she expected. She hadn't spoken the words since throwing them away and moving on to her new, better life. She expected nerves, or sickness, or something pitiful and pathetic when the memories surfaced, but when Salthu settled her golden eyes on her, Ascal felt *understood*.

"Lady of the Dark." Salthu returned her attention to the cobblestone path when they entered Ghizol proper. "That's your title now."

Lady of the Dark.

"Has a nice ring." Ascal smiled and faintly she felt Salthu's grip on her tighten. She felt no desire to stop her.

"Right? So next time we're fighting in the dark, don't get your ass kicked again or you'll embarrass me," Salthu said, lips curling in a teasing grin that had Ascal huffing petulantly.

"You're one to talk," Ascal wriggled in Salthu's hold, glaring at the woman.

"At least I can still walk," Salthu said, grinning.

Ascal rolled her eyes, swallowing a childish huff.

Salthu took her to her home. Ascal had been there a few times before, for dinner or to grab something they needed for the day before Ascal returned to her duties, but she'd never seen Salthu's bed chambers.

She *definitely* hadn't been set on the sheets before.

Salthu stared at her for a moment, eyes boring into hers with a sharp intensity that curled the knot in Ascal's stomach and drew heat down her chest. Salthu opened her mouth to speak, but quickly closed it, her tusks pressing against her upper lip leaving two dimples in their wake.

Adorable.

Ascal curled her fingers into the sheets, swallowing the thick lump in her throat.

"I'm going to get Urzul," Salthu finally said, straightening up and turning on her heel to leave the room.

The sudden departure left Ascal reeling. Alone, Ascal sucked in a breath and exhaled long and loud. *Gods,* what was happening to her? She couldn't understand why looking at Salthu was like gazing into the sun. Bright and fresh and *warm.*

More importantly, why she *liked* the way Salthu made her feel. She hadn't dealt with emotions like that before. She never experienced churning in her stomach outside of eating horrible tavern food. The fluttering in her chest was utterly new and, in some ways, completely terrifying.

There had to be something wrong with her.

She needed a distraction. Pulling herself out of the bed, Ascal groaned when she put weight on her ankle again. She knew it wasn't smart to aggravate the wounds, but she needed something, anything, to do. Snooping would be a decent diversion.

The house was cozy. Warm. Cluttered beyond belief, yet everything had a place and nothing was in the way. The walls were covered in tapestries and pieces of artwork, leaving little of the actual foundation visible. Ascal couldn't place an origin to every item, but she imagined most of them must have come from outside of Ghizol.

As she was inspecting a piece of artwork on the wall, the door opened and an exasperated sigh filled the room.

"Urzul, you might need to sedate her," Salthu said as Ascal turned to face them, though Salthu's fond smile said the threat was empty.

Urzul on the other hand. Ascal could see why Silvyr respected and feared her wrath so much, even as her apprentice. The stern look on her face made Ascal regret ever getting injured in the first place.

"You warriors are ridiculous. In bed, now. You will stay there until you are healed," Urzul commanded, leaving no room for arguments. Not even Ascal was willing to take the chance and hurried back to the bed. "Salthu, get the clothes away from the wound so I can work."

Salthu didn't argue, just jumped to work as ordered. While Urzul set up her salves and braces and bandages, Salthu knelt on the bed beside Ascal, gingerly taking her injured arm. Carefully, intimately, she tore away the fabric around the break, dropping the useless material to the floor. Ascal sucked in a breath, biting the inside of her cheek to contain a yelp each time Salthu moved her arm. It was so much easier to ignore her injuries when someone wasn't moving it around.

"You're staying here until you're healed," Salthu murmured, lifting her eyes for only a moment, gaze intense with unhidden worry, and Ascal found herself nodding without thinking. Only staring into vibrant sunshine.

"Yeah," Ascal replied. Breathless. Baffled. "I'll stay here."

MIGHTIER THAN THE SWORD
TALLI L. MORGAN

Tris was ready when the dragon attacked again.

It had been ten years since it had shown its scaly hide in the town of Valley, and in those ten years Tris had tirelessly trained and worked her way up the ranks until she had earned a place at the Stone Table. *Now* she was a protector of Valley, and it was her responsibility to be prepared for anything. Unlike the common citizens of Valley, who had grown comfortable in their peace and were content to believe the dragon would not return, the knights had never ceased preparing for the inevitable.

Today, dawn brought the inevitable.

"Team Green, get everyone out of the village!" The Commander bellowed instructions from the front of the ranks. "Teams Red, Blue, and Gold—lure the beast away from town. And Team Stone, with me." The Commander secured his helmet on his head and drew his broadsword with a metallic shriek. "Let's take this thing down."

Tris drew her own sword as she fell into position with her fellow knights of Team Stone. The twelve of them followed the Commander to the top of the ridge at the north end of town that acted as a natural barrier between the village and the dragon's realm. Tris took up her spot at the front of the group and waited, pulse thrumming, for the other teams to lead the dragon forward.

The beast perched on the roof of the old stone church, scattering roof tiles with each scrape of its curved talons. Its massive, batlike wings stretched out wide as it opened its jaws and released a bone-rattling shriek. Tris winced, but kept her gaze fixed on the monster and the knights scurrying about beneath it. The colorful capes denoting their teams flapped around them like frantically fluttering wings. The dragon roared again, snapping at the knights, who tripped over each other in their haste to flee out of its bite radius. Tris exhaled a grumble of frustration. *Come on, you're better than this. Get your shit together.*

Team Red was the first to manage that; they pulled away and regrouped, then retreated toward the ridge. The dragon didn't spare them a second glance; its spiked tail whipped in an arc behind it, toppling a few chimneys that had the bad luck of being in its path. Someone from Team Gold launched a spear at the beast; the weapon narrowly missed the fins on the left side of its face, but it was enough to catch the dragon's attention. It shook its head and growled, then reared back with a shriek as another spear soared up and pierced its fin.

Finally, Tris thought. Running in circles in front of the dragon wouldn't catch its attention, but hurting it—even if such a wound was probably equivalent to a paper cut—would anger the beast. And that was precisely what Tris wanted: to fight its rage. Now when Teams Blue and Gold retreated, the dragon followed.

The dragon's wings whipped a gust of wind over the roofs and treetops as it launched itself into the sky. Its clawed feet and sweeping tail ripped up trees and gouged holes in houses on its way over the town; Valley would be a mess in its wake, but stone walls could be repaired. At least the thing hadn't unleashed its fiery breath upon the village.

"Damn good thing we got everyone out," muttered someone behind Tris.

"Should've gotten ourselves out, too," someone else quipped.

"Focus, team," said the Commander. "Get ready."

Tris took a deep breath. Adrenaline pumped strength through her veins. Not a trace of fear made her heart skip or hands tremble. She was ready. This was what she was made for.

"Almost there," warned the Commander. "Steady, team. Steady . . . "

Tris tightened her hands around the hilt of her sword. The other teams dashed up the ridge and took their positions in line behind Team Stone, and not a second too soon. Hardly a heartbeat after the last knight dug in their heels, the dragon swept up with a roar.

The Commander roared back, *"CHARGE!"*

Tris released a bellow of her own and launched herself toward the beast. Her awareness narrowed to two things: the dragon and her blade. *Dodge, swipe, stab, spin.* Sweat and blood ran down her face – the dragon's or hers, she had no idea. Pain and adrenaline rang through her body but her strikes never weakened, her blade never faltered. The sword was and always had been an extension of herself. It was her and she was it. Some days she swore it was magic.

Metal clanged, and knights shouted, and the dragon growled. The fight wore on. Tris landed strike after strike to the dragon's legs, sides, and scaly underside, and though its blood soaked her blade and her armor it did not stumble. She crisscrossed with other knights, swiping at tendons in the monster's ankles; it shook and stomped its feet as if Tris had merely poked it.

Growling through her teeth, Tris spared a glance around the field. Knights darted and floated like bees around the dragon's legs, but Tris couldn't tell if anyone was making a dent in the thing's scales. Though it bled from several wounds along the lower half of its body, it did not seem to care.

How are we supposed to kill this thing? she wondered. Despite her training, she doubted now that such a monster *could* be killed without magic.

"Look out!" Tris snapped out of her thoughts at the shout. She quickly dodged a blow from the dragon's claws, then spun around just in time to shove a fellow Stone knight out of the same deadly path. He stammered a thank-you as he stumbled, but Tris had already returned her focus to the dragon. The other knights' movements around her blurred in her periphery; years of training alongside these people had given her the instincts to trust them. The group fought as a unit, like a pack of wolves. They were like extensions of her just as much as her own blade. They wouldn't give up. Not until this thing was dead.

"*TRIS—*"

The sudden cry from one of the knights shattered her focus and she flinched mid-strike. In her moment of distraction, she failed to see the dragon swipe at her until its claws slammed into her body and launched her off her feet. She hit the ground and rolled, stopping only when a rock blocked her path. Stars popped behind her eyes and a muscle smarted in her shoulder when she tried to roll onto her front side. She gritted her teeth and ignored it, rising to her hands and knees to search for her sword. Her scraped hands found only dirt and rocks, and no amount of blinking successfully cleared the blur from her eyes.

Come on, Tris, get up. You're stronger than this. She pushed herself to her aching knees, then started to get to her feet when another swipe from the dragon sent her tumbling across the dirt again.

Gravity seized her and dragged her down a shallow hill. She opened her eyes in a damp, rocky ravine, and for several pounding seconds all was absolutely still. *Am I dead?* Tris wondered. But no, she could smell the grass and soil, and she could feel every sore inch of her body. The straps of her armor dug painfully into her flesh; the stiff metal plates were not suited for the ragdoll slouch in which she was positioned. She felt made of metal herself, like her joints would creak if she moved.

It was a few minutes before the throbbing pain in her body ebbed enough that she could move; when she finally got herself upright, she realized that the only thing she could hear was her own thundering pulse. The top of the ridge was quiet.

But that was impossible. Where were the other knights? Where was the *dragon*?

Tris dragged herself off the ground, using the sides of the ravine to steady her balance. Gritting her teeth, she climbed up and out of the ravine, and the scene that spread out before her stole the scarce strength she'd recovered. A groan escaped her when her knees hit the dirt.

Her knights—her team—her *family* lay sprawled across the ground with bent limbs and bloodstained armor. Swords and helmets littered the space, broken and flung away from each unmoving body.

Unmoving. All of them. How? How were they all so still?

And the dragon . . .

Tris looked up. The dragon's dark silhouette faded against the sky as it drifted farther and farther away, ascending into the foggy mountain peaks.

On trembling legs, Tris staggered toward the closest body. Eli, a fellow Stone knight whom Tris often dined with. She eased off his helmet, grasping at a faint chance that he might be alive, but the mess of gore that spilled from his throat as his head lolled to the side smothered her hope. Tris recoiled, bile burning at the back of her throat.

She was not awarded any relief by the next fallen knight she turned to. Kas from Team Green, who told the only jokes that made Tris genuinely laugh, had collapsed with their spine twisted and neck snapped. Tris couldn't see their face and she considered that a blessing.

She went to another. Eoin. Team Gold. His eyes, once a deep, rich brown, were glassy and pale and empty.

Another. Kira. Team Stone. The only person other than her blood brother that she considered family. Tris barely recognized her through the blood, viscera, and mangled limbs.

The bodies became blurs in Tris's eyes. She didn't know if she was crying or if her brain had simply decided that she had seen enough. When at last she found the Commander, facedown with a broken neck, torn-off arm, and blood-smeared armor, she collapsed beside his body and broke down. Shudders ran through her, sobs that tore out of her throat but did not force tears from her eyes. She dug her fingers into the hard, rocky dirt beside her Commander's body and threw her head back and screamed.

And screamed.

And screamed.

When her voice broke and gave out and refused to make another sound, Tris gathered the Commander's helmet into her arms and heaved herself to her feet. The mountain fog had swallowed the dragon from sight, but it was up there. Smug and satisfied for now, but it would be back.

If Tris limped home and wallowed in her agony, it would be back. It would never end. All these deaths would be for nothing.

So Tris would see to it that the dragon's reign of terror ended, even if it killed her, too.

Dark had long since fallen when Tris reached the clouds that hugged the mountaintops. There was no question of which peak to climb or how far to go; the dragon had dwelled in the same place as long as anyone could remember. Tris had a map to its lair in her memory. The thing didn't need to hide or relocate. It was a powerful predator, and the citizens of Valley were its prey. It was untouchable.

Tris intended to overturn the monster's smug sense of security.

Exhausted, aching, and bloodstained, Tris staggered into the wide mouth of the dragon's cave. Stalactite teeth loomed over her head, dripping moisture that echoed throughout the cavernous space. It was utterly dark, and Tris had no light to guide her. When the sun had sunk, she had completed her trek by touch alone; up here in the fog, the moonlight did not dare shine.

She did not believe in any gods, and she was skeptical of spirits, but she chose to believe that she had not perished on her journey up here because this was precisely where she was meant to be. This was what she was meant to do. She was a knight of the Stone Table, and she had survived so that she could avenge her fellow knights – and, finally, her brother.

If there was a spirit or a god guiding her, she implored it to strengthen her now.

Tris wrenched her sword out of its scabbard with a sharp, metallic ring. "Dragon! *Monster!* Show yourself. We are not finished."

Deep within the cave, something growled.

"Come on, dragon," Tris coaxed. "Don't you want to finish what you started? I'm the only one you didn't manage to kill!"

Tris hardly recognized her own ragged voice; it was distant in her ears, as were her heavy footsteps over the slick stone. She was numb to the frigid air on her face and the weariness in her bones. Smoky warmth beckoned her deeper into the cave, and with nothing else to guide her, she followed it.

"You're a coward!" Tris shouted at the dark when the monster still refused to show itself. She could hear it breathing and shifting around; its breaths gusted hot wind at her. "Hiding in your cave, all the way up here and out of sight. Pathetic. If I didn't know any better, I'd say you were ashamed of what you've done, but I know you don't have so much as a scrap of care. Get out here and face me, monster!"

Closer than before, the beast's growls vibrated through the stone. Tris heard it move again, claws and scales scraping the rocks. Heavy steps rattled the walls and sent pebbles skittering; Tris shielded her head with her arms as pieces of stone dropped from above. Before her, a massive, steaming shape materialized out of the voidless dark.

Tris gripped her sword and shifted into a stable fighting stance. The sharp scent of copper filled her nose. Heavy, wet, splattering sounds joined the steady drip of water from the cave ceiling; when the dragon lowered its head, dark rivulets of blood leaked from its mouth.

"So we did hurt you," Tris said. "*Good*. You deserve to suffer after everything you've done to us."

The dragon growled, releasing a hot burst of steam from its nostrils. It laid its head down on the stone and closed its fiery eyes. Blood leaked between its interlocked teeth, spraying onto the stone with each of its labored breaths.

"Oh, no. No, no." Tris scoffed. "You don't get to just *die*. Get up and fight, coward." Tris nudged the beast's head with the tip of her sword, but not hard enough to pierce its scales. It winced and twitched its eyes, exhaling a rumbling growl. But still it did not move to strike.

Tris released a growl of her own. "Come on! Get up!" She threw her weight against the side of the dragon's head. At last, it reacted with a halfhearted snap; Tris easily evaded its teeth. She spun around and swung her sword; it collided with and cracked one of the beast's spiraled horns. It groaned and lifted its head up, struggling to a half-upright position with visibly trembling front legs. Blood leaked from crosshatched cuts and slices all around its knees and ankles. It snapped again at Tris, and she made to strike, but a glimpse of something lodged in the dragon's chest interrupted her focus and she let her sword miss.

Tris pivoted to stop her momentum. For a moment she could only stare in shock at the beast; her weapon nearly fell from her hands. The hilt of a sword protruded from the dragon's broad chest, shockingly close to where its heart was armored beneath all those scales, cemented there with congealed blood and broken scales. Only a fraction of the weapon's hilt was visible, the rest having been grown over by scabs and scales desperately trying to heal, but Tris would have recognized that sword anywhere.

It had belonged to her brother, the former Commander. And in his death, the weapon belonged to her. Or it would have, if anyone had been able to recover it from the greedy dragon's hoard.

Anger burned under Tris's skin. The flood of emotions silenced her logic, and before she'd consciously decided her next move, she dropped her sword and hurled herself at the dragon. A running leap brought her level with its heart; her vision tunneled, zeroing in on the embedded hilt of her brother's sword. Her hands grasped it just as gravity reclaimed her, and the force of her falling weight loosened the blade.

But not enough. A twinge of pain shot through Tris's shoulders, but she held fast. The dragon screeched and thrashed, threatening to fling Tris across the cave, but with each erratic movement she felt the blade loosen just a bit more. She gripped the hilt until the bones in her hands ached. She tried to swing her body with the dragon's movement, using her weight and its jerks to free the blade.

Scales crunched and blood squelched. Tris felt it leak over her hands and down her arms, slicking her grip on the sword. The dragon's cries turned to high-pitched whimpers; it moved frantically, throwing itself against the cave walls and violently shaking its body like a wet dog. Tris pulled and writhed with every muscle in her upper body until she lifted her chin above the protruding sword, then braced her feet on the dragon's chest and wrenched it with all her strength.

Give it back. It's mine.

The dragon howled and recoiled just sharply enough that the blade finally came free. Tris hit the floor with a clatter of steel, but miraculously spared herself from slamming her head on the rock. She scrambled to her hands and knees and grabbed her brother's sword, gazing down at it as she caught her breath. Scratched, dulled, and caked in blood and viscera, it was far from the shiny relic it had once been, but steel could be cleaned, and blades could be sharpened. All that mattered was that this heirloom was back in her hands, where it belonged.

For years, Tris had idly entertained the idea of venturing up—into these mountains to retrieve the only remaining piece of her brother, but everyone had told her it was a suicide mission. No one who had tried to reach the dragon's hoard had ever returned, despite numerous efforts to recover the late Commander's prized weapon. But it was more than a trophy or an heirloom to Tris; it was a symbol of her brother's strength—and her own. It was his promise of protection and valor, and that promise was hers to uphold.

Tris swallowed hard against a thick lump in her throat. "I will return victorious, Jory. Valley will be safe under my protection. You did not die in vain."

She gripped the hilt of her brother's sword and shoved to her feet, rounding on the dragon once more. She found, instead, an empty cave.

"What? No!" Tris stormed a few steps forward. Dark, iridescent dragon blood soaked the stone floor, but Tris neither heard nor saw a trace of the monster itself.

"You think this is over?" The cave echoed Tris's voice back to her. "The sword was only half of my prize, you foolish thing. Your *head* is the other half!"

She went deeper into the cave until the dark had swallowed her entirely. "I will get what I came here for, dragon, and I—"

Her feet caught on something in her path that cried out and shrank back. She halted, struggling to see the obstacle in the all-consuming dark, then slowly sank to one knee.

Before her, a whimpering, shivering human form lay huddled beneath a torn and dirty blanket. Tris couldn't see the person's face behind a mop of tangled black hair, but their deathly pale, too-skinny arms that trembled as they hugged their own emaciated body were sign enough that this person needed help. Tris didn't want to imagine the abuse and neglect they had endured.

"Hey, hey . . ." She softened the trained edge from her voice, but admittedly she wasn't great at this kind of thing. Many of the other knights could easily switch back and forth from fierce warrior to soothing caretaker; it was a skill Tris had not yet mastered. She didn't know how to be soft when all her life she had been taught to be a blade.

What was appropriate here? Should she reach out? Hand on the shoulder? Or would that startle the poor soul even more? How long had they been here, imprisoned by that monster?

"It's all right," Tris murmured, then immediately cringed at the words. "Well . . . maybe not. Sorry. You're clearly not all right. But I—"

The person dragged in a ragged breath and turned their head. Their hair fell away from their face, revealing pale cheeks, a sharp jaw, and startlingly bright blue eyes. "No . . . thanks . . . to you."

Tris recoiled. "What?"

With effort, they sat up straighter and the blanket fell away, revealing a gaping wound in the center of their chest. The skin around it had blackened, and it steadily leaked thick, dark blood. Tris was too caught on the impossibility of being *alive* with such a wound to feel any disgust at the gore.

"What happened to you?" Tris's voice wouldn't rise above a shocked whisper.

"You did." The girl bared her teeth in a scowl. Her hands curled around the tattered blanket. "Your village did. Your *knights* did."

This didn't make any sense. Tris had never seen this girl before, and even if she had, why would anyone in Valley—*namely* the knights— harm her? Tris fumbled in the pouches strapped to her belt until she found her matchbook. With trembling fingers, she drew one out and struck it; the flash of light reflected briefly on the injured girl's eyes before she flinched back.

Tris frowned. "You're not human. I don't understand. Who are you?" She studied the girl more closely in the light, and saw now that her skin wasn't lifelessly pale; it was *white*, almost opalescent, with a faint violet undertone. Her blood was dark, with an oily, unnatural shine to it that Tris only knew to exist in . . .

"*You're* the dragon?"

The words sounded stupid even as Tris said them. This was impossible. Dragons weren't shifters, and they weren't *people*. They were monsters, and this one . . .

This one *couldn't* be a suffering, helpless girl. It wasn't fair. This dragon had taken everything from Tris. She had come up here to kill it and take her vengeance. A scared girl in desperate need of help was *not* part of that plan. This had to be a trick. Tris didn't trust it.

The girl let out a hoarse laugh. "You don't believe me. All that logic and experience, and you deny what's right in front of you. I *was* the dragon, but not by choice."

"What, you were cursed or something?" *Convenient excuse,* Tris thought bitterly.

A nod. The girl tipped her head to the side and narrowed her eyes. "By someone who looked quite a lot like you."

Tris's blood ran cold and then hot all at once. She leapt to her feet. "Liar! I won't fall for your tricks! I know how you monsters—"

"You know nothing!" the girl snapped. "And that's exactly the point." She coughed, and blood leaked from her lips. She swiped the back of her hand across her mouth and cleared her throat. "None of you know anything about the creatures and people you call monsters. I ran away from Valley to escape a father that hated me and a life that suffocated me, and the moment I dared show my face near the town, I was hunted. When I sought help after being *stabbed*, I was attacked. I went in peace every single time, and how was I met? With screams and swords. No questions. Just weapons."

"*You* attacked *us,*" Tris pointed out.

"Not until *you* attacked *me.*"

"You destroyed our village!"

"If you had a sword embedded in your chest, I don't think you'd have particularly good depth perception, either."

Tris growled under her breath. Her match burned itself out and she flicked it to the floor, then lit another. The anger bled from the girl's face when the light danced over her again; Tris looked at her now and saw only her pain. Her exhaustion.

"What are you called?" she asked quietly.

The girl blinked, as if that was the last thing she'd expected from Tris's mouth. "Isolde."

"Isolde?" That was a rather uncommon name—an old name—and Tris only knew of one person in Valley who bore it. "Are you . . . *Lady* Isolde? Of House Maroul?"

She blinked a few more times. "Y-Yes, but . . . it seems like it's been a very long time since anyone called me that."

"Indeed," muttered Tris. "You've been missing for years."

"Years . . ." Isolde brought her knees up to her chest and hugged her arms around them.

Tris shifted uncomfortably on her feet. "I'm Tris," she said for lack of anything better to say. She sank to her knee again and snuffed out the match. In the minute it took for her vision to adjust to the dark, neither of them said anything. Tris didn't know what to do. There was no longer a dragon, no longer something to fight, but she couldn't just walk away. This girl needed help. But would she even accept assistance from Tris, or anyone else in Valley? Would she forgive them for hurting her?

Did they deserve that forgiveness? Did Tris?

And what if it was true—that Jory, honored Commander and Tris's beloved brother—had been the one to plunge that sword into this girl's chest?

Tris couldn't find anything to refute that truth. It was Jory's sword, undeniably, that Tris had pulled from the dragon's body. But Tris knew her brother; underneath his armor, he had been kind and loving. He would not have attacked if he could have helped. But he had likely seen only a monster—something to fight, a threat to eliminate.

"Who was he? The man who looked like you." Isolde hugged her knees tighter. "The one who stabbed me."

"My brother," Tris said.

Isolde winced. "I'm sorry."

"Don't be. Gods know you have nothing to be sorry for. We're the ones who hurt you."

Isolde narrowed her eyes. "You changed your mind on that rather quickly."

"Do you not want me to believe you?" Tris huffed. "I know what we did to you. I was there. And the times I wasn't there, I heard a detailed report. An apology won't fix what we've done, but will you still let me help you? I can't... I can't just leave you like this."

"Why should I trust you?" Isolde said. "You came up here to kill me."

"I came up here to kill a dragon," Tris said softly. "And I don't see a dragon. Do you?"

Isolde frowned. "No. Not anymore. And I guess I have you to thank for that."

"How long were you under that curse?" Tris searched her memory, but she couldn't pinpoint when the daughter of Valley's lord had gone missing. It was long enough that everyone had stopped talking about it, but not so long that Lord Maroul had declared her deceased. Still, if Tris had to guess, it had been at least eight years. Lady Isolde had been a child when she'd disappeared, and though it was hard to judge this girl's age thanks to her poor health, Tris could believe she was around seventeen.

Isolde shrugged, shaking her head. "I don't know. I started to lose memories of . . . before. Things are still coming back to me. There were times when I didn't know I'd ever been human at all. It was frightening."

"I'm sorry," Tris murmured. She gave Isolde space to say more, and when she didn't, Tris pulled off her cloak and draped it around the girl's shoulders. "Here. It's freezing out there. I'm sorry I can't give you more, but when we return—"

"Return?" Isolde frowned. "To Valley?"

"Y-Yes?" Tris was confused. "Don't you want to . . . go home?"

"To the place that hunted and tried to kill me?" Isolde pulled the cloak tighter around her body. "No. Valley is not my home."

"Wh—You can't stay in this cave!"

"Why not?"

Tris stared at her. "You'll freeze? Among other things?" She sighed. "Isolde, please. Let me help you. I—I need to help you, after what I did." And after what Jory had done, too.

"Bringing me to Valley would not help me," Isolde said. "It would help *you*. You don't need to help me for my own good; you only want to help me so you'll feel better about *this*." She parted the cloak to expose the wound in the center of her chest. Tris winced. Isolde crossed her arms. "Valley hasn't been my home in a long time. I ran away, all those years ago, and I do not intend to go back."

Tris didn't know what to do. Again. She always had a solution; she rarely faced a problem she didn't know how to fix. She did not like that she was seemingly powerless here. "Then what do you want? What can I do?"

"Now you're asking the right questions." Isolde flickered a smile. "I want to be free. You've freed me from the curse, sure, but I want to be free of all the rest, too."

Tris frowned. "What do you mean?"

"When you go back to Valley, I want you to tell everyone that the dragon is dead. And so is Lady Isolde."

"But—But what are you going to do?" Tris refused to leave this girl here to die. Even if she wanted to – which until a second ago, did not seem to be the case—Tris wouldn't allow it. She had a duty to the people of Valley, missing ones included.

Isolde smiled. "I'm going to be free."

"Isolde—"

"Tris." Isolde rose to her feet and let the cloak fall in a heap around her ankles. When Tris went to grab it, Isolde shook her head. She pressed her hands over the wound on her chest and closed her eyes.

Tris watched, stunned, as Isolde slowly skimmed her hands along her torn skin and seamlessly healed it. In seconds there was no evidence of her injury. Isolde inhaled a deep breath, tipping her head back, then breathed out and opened her eyes.

"I was never free at home," she said. "My father kept me cooped up, isolated from everyone but him. He brought me out to show off to the other aristocrats in Valley, but all the while he forced me to suppress who I really am. I was a trophy, a doll."

Tris shook her head. That was no life.

"My memories are foggy," Isolde continued. "But I think he was the one who cursed me. And I know *this* is why."

She spread out her arms, and in a blink of blue light, Isolde became a bird. Instead of a girl, Tris now knelt before a white dove with light blue streaks in its feathers. It fluttered its wings a few times, then cocked its head to peer up at Tris.

If she had not witnessed the transformation with her own eyes, she would not, in a thousand years, believe this. Tris had seen small magics done before, but nothing like this. She knelt on the ground and gazed in wonder at the little bird. "Isolde? That's really you?"

"It is." She ruffled her wings. "This is the reason my father shut me away. He could not understand or accept that I can shift my form. It scared him. So he forbade me from doing it, and when he caught me shifting anyway, he . . . threatened me. He locked me in my chambers for three days, and I knew things would only get worse if I didn't get out of there. I ran away. I transformed into the dragon so I could defend myself—and so everyone would leave me alone. But the moment I was spotted outside Valley . . . well, you know what happened next. One good stab to the chest and my power became a curse: I got stuck as the dragon."

Tris's heart ached. She'd had no idea Lady Isolde had been treated like this; then again, nothing had ever made her pay attention. Lord Maroul and his wealthy circles were outside of the world Tris knew, and if she had ever seen Lady Isolde at all it was more likely to be in portraits than in person. But how many people who had been near her hadn't paid attention? Or worse, how many of them had known of her father's abuse and remained silent?

No wonder the girl didn't wish to return.

Tris knew it wasn't her fault, but she still felt like she'd failed, somehow. Her duty was to protect the citizens of Valley, and that included its nobility. She *should* have been paying attention.

"Now that I haven't got a blade stuck in my chest, I can go anywhere," Isolde said. "I can shift freely and be anything and anyone I want." Another blink of blue light, and Isolde stood in her human form once again—now healthier, fleshed out, and clothed in a long, pale blue robe. Her brown hair fell in waves down her back, and her eyes—still that stunning blue—were brighter now. She looked older than Tris had originally thought, closer to twenty than seventeen.

Tris gazed up at Isolde and found herself smiling. She pressed her fist to her chest, then bowed her head as she would to show deference and devotion to a higher-ranking knight.

"Oh– Tris, please stand."

"Isolde," Tris murmured, thinking it best to omit her title, "I failed to protect you when you needed it most. When you were suffering and needed help, I caused you harm instead. This breaks every oath I have ever sworn, and I shall never do so again. I give you my word that I shall not speak of our meeting here, nor shall I betray to anyone I meet that you are alive and free. This will be between us. This I promise to you."

"Tris . . . " Isolde's voice was soft, perhaps a bit choked up. She knelt to Tris's level and gently touched her cheek, tilting her head up. "You are honorable. You are kind. You've given me my life back, and for that you will forever have my gratitude. Should you need anything at all that I can give, you need only ask."

Tris met Isolde's eyes. "We'll meet again, then?"

Isolde smiled. "I should hope so."

Tris took her hand and pressed a kiss to the back of it, then bowed her head again. When she rose, Isolde rose with her; their hands lingered together, reluctant to part. Isolde flickered a gentle smile, then drew away from Tris and shifted with a flash of blue light. She became an owl, snowy feathers spotted with periwinkle. She stretched her wings, then with a flurry of feathers she launched herself toward the mouth of the cave.

Tris hurried after her, following the whoosh of wings until she could see beyond the cave's darkness. Isolde was a spot of white against a starry black sky, rising on the wind.

Though Tris's heart felt lighter, she also couldn't help but feel like she had just lost something she hadn't known she'd wanted. It seemed like ages since she'd fought the dragon outside of Valley, and yet her moments with Isolde felt like fleeting glimpses of a dream. So many things had changed so quickly. Tris had come up here to kill a dragon. Instead, she'd found someone who needed help. And Tris *had* helped her, by breaking the curse but also by letting her go. Still, Tris selfishly didn't want it to be over so soon.

She had given Isolde what she'd needed—she knew this—so why did she *still* feel like she'd failed?

She would return to Valley empty-handed. No, she would not have the dragon's head. Nor would she take her brother's sword, or even her own. She would return with only the memory of this night and the promise she'd made. No trophies. No proof of her victory.

And maybe that was okay. Maybe not every victory needed a trophy. Maybe sometimes, victories could be quiet things.

Tris would return home to a town in shock. All of her fellow knights were dead. There was no Commander, there were no ranks or teams. She was alone.

Coming back to face that, no one would expect loud triumph from her. And though she would rather have her teams alive, she found relief knowing that her return would bring gratitude that she had survived. And the dragon would not hurt any of them ever again.

She had promised.

OILBACK BEETLE SYMBIOSIS

DEWI HARGREAVES

The people of the Burikol clan followed the oilback beetle herds wherever they went, and they never looked Backward.

The oilback beetles had an innate sense for when it was time to move. Their heavy chittering heads would raise and they would clatter their vast, oily elytra, communicating with each other in their secret language, and the next day they would plod onwards, and the Burikolish would have no choice but to pack up quickly and trek after them, following until they stopped again. The sound of their language was one they were well used to; it could be heard a mile or more away, echoing on the wind. In the old times, the beetles had used it to keep the herd together.

The priests said the giant beetles were blessed with the gift of foreordination—they knew the future, and this made them a gift from the gods. The more practically minded said the beetles had a sixth sense the Burikolish could not comprehend. The truth didn't matter: either way, the oilbacks knew when danger was coming and they moved away from it—so by following them, they too avoided danger. It was an arrangement that had worked for countless generations.

The Burikolish had been following the beetles on a long march into unknown land for nigh-on six months. On the beasts went, plodding inexorably, their metal shoes clanking on the dry ground. They had never walked this long, nor this far. Some of the leaders were worried.

Drisoli looked over the valley below. Dusty earth stretched as far as he could see. Stark shadows fell across the landscape, cast by the day's dying sun. Outcrops of craggy cliffs and gullies emerged from the ground in places, only to be reabsorbed some few hundred yards later. They gave Drisoli the impression there was a huge monster of stone beneath them that had been buried by sand and dirt over millennia, leaving only the extremities visible.

The oilbacks had led them over a mountain range of red stone. It had been a gruelling journey and several of their clan were now strapped to the beetles' backs, too tired to walk further. The scouts had promised they would find a water source soon, but the new valley looked even more barren than the last.

Drisoli looked at the scout standing beside him. "No water," he said.

The scout shrugged, their face hidden behind their dust mask. "The beetles must drink eventually. They know these places better than we."

Drisoli wondered why they had scouts if they didn't know the terrain, but it was not his place to question the ways of the clan. Rumours swirled that they had lost a couple of oilbacks two nights ago —they had simply disappeared—and people were restless. The herd never split.

He did not want to cause any further disturbance with his insolent words.

Drisoli was a simple milker, which had been determined by the position of the stars on the night he was born. It was his job to drain fluid from the beetles—the sticky, shiny jelly they used for cooking and brewing. Over many years, Drisoli had honed his craft. He was now Head Milker, which earned him some respect in the clan.

As such, when they stopped and made camp for the night, he was summoned to the leader's tent to decide what they should do.

The leader's tent was heavy with the sweet smoke of the long pipes they so loved, into which they poured a tar-like mix of beetle jelly and tangleaf. The smoke clung to his tongue, at once bitter and sugary, and dried the inside of his nostrils.

Obstetsterix, the elderly leader of the Burikol clan, sat on his clanstool, which was carved from beetle shell, and surveyed his makeshift council through narrowed eyes. His robes were intricately woven from some silk they'd bought from a clan of nomadic worm tamers. He wore a cap carved from shell, lacquered with a jelly varnish and inked with bright patterns of yellow and blue. The shadows cast by the central fire made him look intimidating, almost otherworldly, like a herald of the gods come to oversee them.

Drisoli was tired. The day had already been long, and he dreamed of nothing more than creeping back to his own modest tent and snuggling in beside Hyltri.

The discussion was already underway.

Many of the aristocratic families had grouped together as the Traditionalists; they argued they should trust the instincts of the oilbacks, as they always had. They wanted to follow the herd without question, knowing that to do so was to follow the will of the gods themselves. "Our people never go Backward," they thundered. The scouts had joined them, as had the pilots who drove the beetle herds. It was a strange contrast—these lithe young warriors in their practical garb standing alongside the venerable heads of the older families, decked out in finery passed down through generations.

On the other side of the tent, the Contrarians gathered. They said the creatures may have lost their way—or worse, perhaps the beetles had decided the Burikolish were no longer useful. For all time, their two species had lived in symbiosis, but some argued they were more of a burden than a benefit to the oilback beetles and the beetles would one day try to escape. The Contrarians believed that time had now come. The beetles were leading them on a death march to nowhere, and the clan's only chance of survival was to abandon them and strike out on their own.

This debate had raged every night for a month or more, with no progress or conclusion. Drisoli sat in the corner as they bickered once again, half-asleep and not paying much attention, as he had so many nights before.

Obstetsterix stood suddenly, clasping his hands. All conversation stopped.

"It seems we have reached an impasse," the old man said. "All have chosen their side, and neither has the majority. There is but one leader who has remained quiet."

They all knew who he meant. The crowd parted, leaving a long corridor between the clan leader and Drisoli, who blinked in surprise.

"Me?" he spluttered. "Surely you cannot mean me. I am but a milker."

"A well-respected milker," Obstetsterix said.

"Your voice commands weight amongst the commons," a haughty member of the Traditionalists said, his bright red hair bound in a bun.

"People love a working politician," a Contrarian agreed. "Someone who gets stuck in and labours by their side."

"It seems we have a majority opinion," Obstetsterix said, smiling. "You shall have the deciding vote."

"You're voting to… give me the vote?"

"Yes," the elderly leader said, his smile never faltering. "Otherwise, we may kill each other in this very tent."

As darkness fell across the camp, Drisoli made his way home.

The camp's core was home to the noble families. Their elaborate tents, surrounded by smaller dwellings for their sokemen, were like little villages in themselves, each covered in family symbols to mark their territory.

Drisoli worked his way outwards, following the makeshift paths that would disappear when they packed up the next morning. His modest tent stood near the outermost ring. He had recently upgraded; he and Hyltri now had two rooms, a sleeping quarters and a living quarters, something of which he was very proud. He planned to purchase a young oilback triungulin from one of the richer families once they had saved enough, so they could make jelly of their own.

Hyltri waited outside, stirring a pot of something delicious over the fire.

Drisoli leaned in and kissed him softly. "Smells beautiful, darling."

Hyltri cocked his head. "What's happened?"

"Nothing," Drisoli said, entering the tent.

Hyltri followed him. "I know you well enough by now," he said softly. His fingers slowly tested Drisoli's hand, searching for permission. Drisoli opened his palm, and they linked hands.

Drisoli turned, looking into his partner's eyes. They held concern.

"Something happened at the council," Hyltri said, flicking his long brown hair out of his face. "Have they made a decision?"

"They have," Drisoli said.

"So what's it to be? We soldier on? Or we turn our course?"

"They've given that responsibility to me," Drisoli said. "Tie-breaking vote."

"That's not fair," Hyltri said, his eyes flashing. "Whatever happens, it'll be on your head. They'll blame any misfortune on you."

"I fear that's their plan," Drisoli said, and slunk off to bed.

Half an hour later, Hyltri followed wordlessly. He brought a bowl of steaming soup, which Drisoli took thankfully, and hugged Drisoli tight—tighter than the night before—when they settled down to sleep.

The sun rose over a blossom-pink world and Drisoli went to milking.

Hyltri gave him a little kiss as he left and squeezed his hand. "I trust your judgement," he said. "I will follow you."

The camp moved. They shuffled along the valley like a tick across some enormous beast's back. They passed beneath barren outcrops, though they eventually found life: a wall of lichen as tall as a hundred tents or more stretched up a cliff face, a riot of bright yellows, blues and oranges in the wasteland. They stopped for a while. Folks gathered lichen for cooking and oilbacks grazed lazily before the pilots eventually urged them on.

Drisoli spent the morning milking, draining the underbellies of the beetles with special silver tools.

One of the oilbacks kicked a milker away, grunting angrily. It happened sometimes. They restrained her until she had calmed down and completed the procedure. Sometimes it was painful—they were using blades, after all—but the incisions were shallow, and their bellies were well-padded with fat. It was something they had been doing for generations. It was safe.

Drisoli kept his new council-given responsibilities a secret from the rest of his team. To them, he was still just Drisoli the Head Milker, and that gave him some comfort. He decided to question them subtly about what they should do next, to get an idea of the general feeling amongst the common folk of the clan.

"What do you think we should do?" he asked Roaes, the oldest milker—a short, slight woman with wild hair.

"We follow the beetles," she said piously. "We always have, we always will. They're leading us this way for a reason. I feel it in my gut. We have to stay the course."

"And if we don't find any water?"

"We will find water," she said resolutely. "The beetles know. We Burikolish never go Backward. It's worked for centuries."

After, he went to speak to Ayap, who he'd always thought of as a very practical, irreverent workman. Ayap snorted and spat on the ground as Drisoli asked the question, then rubbed his hands together.

"Ask me, there ain't nothing special about those beetles. No more special than the thousands of ants and spiders we trample over every day, 'cept they're bigger, stronger, and they taste nice. Perhaps they've lost their way. Walking towards the cliff like sheep or lemmings. But I don't put much stock in the gods, or prophecy, or foreord... foreordinian... you know. They're just beetles," he concluded, picking the end of his nose.

Drisoli left the conversation feeling dejected. Whatever course of action he chose, it seemed he would upset half the clan. He would be blamed, and who knew how far it would go if things got much worse? The shellspears had not been used in many years, but they were still sharp, and they were still strapped to the flanks of the beetles, their shafts rattling as they plodded along, reminders of the Burikolish people's warlike past.

Drisoli dreamt of war that night. He dreamt of burning tents, of fleeing children, of oilbacks yowling at the sky and shaking their elytra, their flanks pierced by hunting spears. The sky burned red and the God of Battle laughed, a hollow sound that somehow echoed across the world and in Drisoli's throat.

He woke drenched in sweat, the blankets down by his feet. Hyltri was curled up at the far end of the tent, watching him.

When Drisoli calmed down, he invited Hyltri back and his comforting touch got him through the night.

For countless years, a witch had shadowed their camp.

She lurked about three days behind them, just on the edge of viewing. Scouts often saw the smoke from her fire. They would occasionally hear the mating calls of her oilbacks when it was the season. But none spoke of her, and none spoke to her. She was an outcast. She had Walked Back.

It was a sin to retrace one's steps. Life, the priests told them, was a continuous line, experienced in order from start to finish. To trace one's steps was a great evil, an attempt to upset the course of the universe. The witch had Walked Back, so now she was shunned.

Some feared this twisting of the universe had given her a strange power. The ability to see the future, or at least to better understand the past and predict the future because of that. As much as this discomforted most of the Burikolish, it enticed others to seek her out. According to rumour, anyway. None who had Walked Back had ever returned.

When he woke, Drisoli found the camp in a febrile mood. "Another day without water," folks were grumbling. Traditionalists lurked in dark corners, glaring balefully at any who passed. Contrarians marched between tents, banging drums and blowing flutes, spreading their warning as loudly as possible.

"I reckon you have mere days left," a herald from Obstetsterix told him.

It made Drisoli shiver.

When he returned from milking, he pecked Hyltri's cheek as usual. They chewed their way through dried meat and nuts—with water running so low they could no longer afford the luxury of cooking soup.

When they'd eaten, he began throwing provisions in a large satchel.

"Where are you going?" Hyltri asked him.

His throat dry and his heart pounding, his reply was quiet. "Backward."

Hyltri's eyes grew wide. "Backward? But why? What for?"

"I must consult the witch."

"She's mad," Hyltri insisted. "You'll find no answers there. You'll just waste more time. And everyone in camp will shun you."

"Not if I come back with a solution."

"You're so sure?"

"People are desperate," Drisoli insisted as he placed a pouch of berries in the satchel and hoisted it over his shoulder. "Desperate people take desperate action."

"I'm desperate not to lose you," Hyltri said suddenly, stepping forward and taking his hands. "Nor the life we've worked so hard to build here."

Hyltri glanced around their tent at their pots and pans, their dishes and forks—even some scrolls that held songs, a rare luxury—and heaved a heavy sigh. He said nothing, but Drisoli knew what he was thinking. With neither of them in camp to mind their stuff, it would be treated the same as the belongings of the dead or the banished. Their goods would be seized and given to whoever needed them most.

When Drisoli walked out, he walked alone.

Drisoli's shoulder hurt.

He looked back across the wide expanse, spying the dark stain that was the Burikolish camp—which had been, until that morning, the only life he had ever known.

It was strange being alone. His whole life he'd been used to the bustle of people around him, the gentle shuffle of the giant beetles, the padding of many feet across dusty ground. To be alone was uncomfortable in an apocalyptic sense; he felt detached, as though the world outside his immediate experience had ceased to be.

It was deeply unnerving, and he longed for it to be over.

The calls of the oilbacks reverberated round the valley, distorted by craggy rock faces.

The satchel was heavy, and the strap was boring into his skin. He adjusted his shoulder uncomfortably, shifting the bag to his other arm.

You can't go Backward, a voice told him. He smiled bitterly.

He wondered if his people had misunderstood their own teachings and taken the meaning of 'Backward' too literally.

He climbed higher into the hills, heading towards the mountains they had descended several days ago. Rock turned from white to sandy brown to a deep, oxidised red. A single wisp of smoke was his beacon, the only tether connecting him to the world.

When he pitched his tent and settled for the night, he felt more lonely than ever.

Every night, the Burikolish gathered around firepits and sang. Their songs were loud and raucous. They would drink beetle jelly wine and dance. They would embrace and laugh and, when night fell, take their chosen partners to their tents, because the Burikolish never slept alone.

He sat in his tent cross-legged and listened. The only sound was the whisper of the wind. Even the beetles were silent. He tucked under his blankets and curled up against the cold, allowing tears to spill down his cheeks.

Ever since they had first chosen each other, he and Hyltri had not spent a night apart. Some in the clan thought them weird for it—most had several favourites—but it gave him comfort, a stable ground to build from. Now that ground was gone.

You cannot go Backward.

On the second day, his shoulder pain grew worse. The sun was hotter than before and sweat coated his body, slickening his skin and soaking his clothing, making it heavier.

The incline was steeper. Several times he lost his footing amongst the loose rocks, sending them skittering back down the slope. Later, he found himself inching along a narrow walkway, edged by sheer rock on his left and a sharp plummet on his right. He froze, momentarily stricken by the enormity of his situation, paralysed and unable to go on. It was those words that steadied him, that made him take a tentative step, then another, and another. *You cannot go Backward*, he thought, and he knew that his clan misused those words. They were an urge to bravery, not fear. Exploration, not isolation.

When he made camp that night, he was near delirium from exhaustion. The wind howled, boughing the walls of his tent and threatening to bring it crashing down on him. He dreamt that Hyltri came to find him and Drisoli sent him away, screaming at him, telling him not to abandon all they'd built, that he should live comfortably where he could not. Hyltri left, tears drawing clear lines in his dust-stained cheeks. The wind blew harder, casting his tent from the cliffs. It glided on the air currents like a leaf, drifting gently down, away, away, from both camp and witch, with him clinging to it for life, his fingers aching.

He woke panting, unable to tell reality from dream.

On the third day, Drisoli continued the ascent. His calves burned and his mouth was dry. His head swam and he began to wonder if he had enough stamina to get back home once this was done. *You cannot go Backward.*

The sun was blisteringly hot. The ground scorched his feet. When he heard an oilback's cry of pain, he first thought he was hallucinating.

The cries continued as he ascended, growing louder. He stopped close to the witch's smoke plume, his skin prickling. The trail was blocked by a pair of oilbacks lying prone, their legs tucked up beneath them.

He immediately ran to them, placing a hand on one's head. It shivered slightly and recoiled from his touch. He pulled back in shock, giving the creature space. He'd never known one to respond to his touch with fear.

"Leave them be," came a voice from above.

Standing atop an outcrop of rock was a lone figure in a long, thin robe, her silhouette black against the sun. He knew who she was.

He stepped back as commanded and knelt with one hand on his waist and the other on his neck, the posture of submission.

The witch laughed. "Get up, you fool. I mean you no harm."

He stood, looking back at the beetles. "What happened to them?" he asked.

"They're exhausted," she said. "Don't fear. I have treated them, and they will recover. They will find their way back to your camp in time."

His eyes widened. "They belong to us?"

"These and many others," the witch said. "Come, follow. My tent is not far, and you look half way to death."

Drisoli did not need further convincing.

The air within the witch's tent was mercifully cool. It was full of clutter —here a set of drums, there a pile of cooking pots, many chipped or rusting. Chimes hung outside and they rang every time the wind blew, making a surprisingly deep and mournful sound, like the cry of a lost spirit.

The witch was shorter than Drisoli had imagined. She was thin, her waist almost disappearing beneath her intricate robes. She moved slowly, with a calculated air. The rumour was that in her day she had been a fearsome fighter who rode great warbeetles into battle, but to look upon her now, stirring the food over her cooking fire with a kindly expression on her face, he couldn't imagine it.

"You have sacrificed much to come here," she said.

Drisoli deflected. "You are not far behind us. We always see your smoke, and we can almost see the camp from your ridge. It was a short journey."

"You know that's not what I mean," she said, her back to him. She lifted a spoonful of soup to her lips, testing it carefully. "Do you want some?"

Drisoli's stomach rumbled. He had not eaten in days. But he knew he could not trust the witch, so he politely declined.

She shrugged and ate another spoonful.

"You said there were others," he said. "More oilbacks. What did you mean?"

"My oilbacks listen to the clattering of their brethren," she said. "They report their words back to me. Occasionally we find them injured. We restore them."

"You understand them?" he asked, hardly believing her.

"Oh, yes," she said with a dismissive wave. "It's just like learning any other language. Except I can't speak it, only listen. I have no elytra, as you may have noticed."

"What do they tell you?"

She smiled enigmatically. "You will learn, but you must try the soup."

Reluctantly, Drisoli approached the cauldron. The soup was viscous, dripping thickly from the spoon like treacle. It popped and bubbled, a dark brown sludge that smelled like caramelised onions and summer fruits—and something else vaguely sweet and pungent that he couldn't identify. The strange combination made his stomach roil.

The witch slid up behind him, smelling of fresh flowers. She laced her fingers around his waist. "Do it," she whispered.

He took the spoon and filled his mouth.

Instantly, the world began to spin, as though they were seized by a tornado. He felt unsteady and braced against the cauldron briefly for stability, then retracted his hands from the hot rim with a hiss of pain.

"Take my hand," the witch said somewhere behind him.

He spun to find her, but couldn't. She was in three places, five, seven, and always twisting.

"Now!"

Ten hands reached out, and he grasped one.

When he opened his eyes, Drisoli screamed.

The earth was far below. The trail of smoke from the witch's hut was as narrow as a hair, and the mountains sprawled away like splats of paint on canvas. The Burikolish camp was little more than a black mark.

Drisoli flailed, expecting to fall, but found that he was gliding steadily. The witch hovered at his side, her eyes sparkling with amusement.

"Follow me," she said.

They flew along the trail the clan had followed over the last two months, skirting through valleys, down gullies and between mountain ranges, across endless drylands. To his surprise, they passed several patches of green—areas of verdant plant life surrounding oases or rivers. All were just out of view of the path they had taken—tucked away at the ends of valleys or hidden behind hills.

Drisoli's heart sank. "They missed the water…"

More than once. It wasn't an accident.

"Were the beetles testing us? Seeing how far our loyalty stretched?" Drisoli asked. "How resilient we are? Why didn't they lead us to the water?"

"A little of all three, I think," the witch said, her hair blowing as they hovered. She tucked her feet up beneath her.

"They aren't fleeing a disaster, as far as I can tell. Could they be preparing for a future one? Maybe. Could they be trying to escape you? Force you away? Possible too. Perhaps they are sick of how you drain the stuff meant for their young from their bellies."

Drisoli bristled. His whole profession revolved around milking the beetles. "What do you mean?"

She gestured for him to follow, swooping low over the land. Day and night flew by in seconds. They found themselves before an oilback sitting on the path, legs tucked up. It sat there for days, shivering, before the witch and her pack of beetles came to retrieve it. Drisoli recognised the creature by the unique marks on her shell and felt a wrench of shame in his gut.

"This was my doing," he said.

"The symbiosis means that, for better or worse, they are your world.

You cannot survive without them. You must protect them, nurture them. You cannot fight them. And right now, I worry you are killing them."

"How did we lose the beetle? We always count the herd."

The witch had an ashen look. "Never look Backward," she said quietly. "Perhaps you should learn to stay in place sometimes, watch the world go by." She turned to him as darkness fell once more. "Actually *listen* to these creatures you claim to worship. You might learn something."

When Drisoli opened his eyes, he found himself back in the witch's tent. He felt uneasy.

He could not go back to his old life. Not knowing what he knew now. He saw the truth for the first time, saw his people for what they were. Naïve, dangerously so. Not only harming themselves, but also the world around them. But where to go from here?

"You have a choice," the witch said, as though she knew his thoughts. "You can return to the clan, try to change their ways. You can stay here. Or," she said, with emphasis, "you can follow your own path. Either way, use what you've learned to make change."

Drisoli shook his head, his stomach clenching with fear. He didn't want this. He never wanted this. He was just a milker. These were decisions to be made by clan leaders, not dairy farmers.

He wanted his companion. The ground beneath his feet, the warmth in his cold night. "I cannot do this without Hyltri."

The witch smiled cheekily. A shadow fell across the tent's door. Drisoli turned to see Hyltri standing there—dusty, sweaty, his hair matted, but his lips splitting into a wide grin.

Drisoli ran to him, and they embraced, and Hyltri, the much taller of the two, lifted him off his feet. "Did you really think I'd let you leave me behind?" he asked.

They enjoyed each other's company for a long while. The witch made tea for them, which calmed Drisoli and gave him the clarity of mind he needed to look to the future. Eventually, after more tea and some dry biscuits for the road—generously gifted by the witch—they were ready to leave.

Drisoli paused in the tent's awning, looking back over his shoulder. The witch had returned to stirring her pot.

"What do you think I should do?" he asked.

"That is down to you," she said. "But I will say this: I think we can learn something from looking backward from time to time," she said with an encouraging smile. "It's how I discovered so much."

TO CAGE A GODKILLER
AMANDA FERREIRA

There's a smell that lingers in old, abandoned taverns, like ambition once glorious turned sour and doubtful. That makes it easy to bottle; I just pull out the cork, rake a vial through the air, and the ghost of a long-dead adventurer clinging to the rafters coalesces into a deep, radiant purple within the glass, doubling over like a trapped will-o-wisp.

If I had the power, I'd take more than one at once, but this caging alone sucks all the magic from my skin, the runes on my arms and legs burning away until nothing remains. I'd have to repaint them all, stroke by stroke, with heart-oak sap I can no longer afford, so this is all I can do. For now.

"Hurry up," my companion complains from the doorway, his hood already drawn, his long, tawny tail tucked anxiously around the back of his leg. When he turns towards me, I can just make out the fine lines of his whiskers and mane, a golden yellow that even the shadows of his hood do little to hide. "You're dragging this out on purpose."

"Do *you* want to catch them?" I taunt back, and he laughs, his smile all teeth and nerves. On the floor between my feet, the sole candle he'd lit with a snap of his fingers splutters once and goes out, dropping the temperature in the room like a cloud blocking the sun. It's as sure a sign as any; the ghosts here are restless, unmoored. They need me, even if they don't know it yet.

"I'll be back," I whisper into the room, and the blackened wood of the stairwell, bar, ceiling, and floor groan back. There's no furniture left here, not even a door—that was all stolen long ago, with whatever else could be salvaged after a fire mostly destroyed this place—but what little remains still remembers. Still waits.

Outside, the chill of the evening air has cooled with the press of nightfall, the shadows hungry as they bleed out from the trees. I try not to step into the darkest pools, crisscrossed by fallen leaves, but it's impossible. Within minutes, I'm shivering even in my fur-lined boots.

"Come here," Hadrian offers, "you're freezing," but the weight of his arm across my shoulders slows our run. We try to make it work, his body warm against mine, but after a few steps I'm forced to break away, the darkness filling the empty space between us like a living thing.

"It's okay, we're almost there."

It's my third lie tonight, and I hate that I've kept count. Hadrian has only ever been kind and welcoming since meeting me, and despite how badly I stick out in his crew of rogue enchanters, he's vouched for me at every turn. *Pella was top of her class at the academy. Pella works harder than anyone I know. Pella can outshoot any of us with a bow. Pella truly wants to help people.*

All lies, of course. Even my name is something I stole from a ghost —a victim of the monster I've trapped in my bow, his secrets burned under my fingernails like blood I can't wash away. He was the first ghost I trapped, and the reason I can't stop trapping others. He's the only reason I'm worth anything at all.

As if on cue, my quiver grows heavy, the weight seeming to double against my back. It's like a phantom limb that's still attached to me, forever aching, forever calling.

"Pella," Hadrian finally says, and the name suits me, when he says it. *Pea-La.* His mouth holds the vowels perfectly, even in his shifted form as he runs.

He points towards the ground, to where the path we'd been following dissolves into rotten tree roots and crushed leaves, turned black and blue by the hour. The forest is dense here, so dense the air tastes lifeless and stale. "Didn't you say—"

"Here," I repeat, then point even further on, further away. I have to find an open space; any meadow or glade will do. "I know it's here."

He thinks we're looking for a teleportation circle, bone white and stark in the moonlight, hidden from casual passersby behind a simple illusionary spell. I can sense it, somewhere on my right, like there's a string tied to my pinkie that connects me to the runes. But I keep turning left, leading Hadrian deeper into the forest, until I find the perfect place to stop.

He'll forgive me, for tonight. He has to.

But when he touches my arm, so gentle and reassuring that it catches my breath, it fills me with guilt that doesn't belong to me, foreign and hot.

I look at him—look at my friend, my ally, my confidante—weighing my decision.

In his animal form, more lion than man, Hadrian is nearly a foot taller than me, though he tries his best to hide it. He hunches in on himself, tucking his fur and his claws and his tail into his cloak like they horrify him—or he's afraid they horrify others.

The other enchanters in his party are shifters too, but none of them grow as big as he does during a full moon. Even his half-sister, a few years his senior, only comes up to my shoulder when she shifts, though the fierceness of her gaze more than makes up for what her height lacks.

Hadrian isn't like them; not when it comes to me. He's never questioned what I do with the ghosts I trap or why I travel so far to find them. It makes what I'm about to do all the worse.

"You can tell me if we're lost," he says. The deep timber of his voice rattles out of his chest like the echo in a cave. His throat is meant to roar, his words meant to carry. Whispering suits him as poorly as his human clothes, which fit him badly in the chest and the thighs, stretching tight against his fur. "I can try to find the way."

He can *try*, but the pull on my pinkie is so faint I have to hold my breath to feel it there, guiding me home. Without me to find it, he'd be stuck here, and the walk back to camp would kill him; it's more than a thousand miles away.

"Cheer up," I offer softly, and when I pat him on the shoulder, he smiles again, his hood dropping back from his face. His ears are small and curved, a light pink on the inside, partially buried in his mane.

I strike him, just then, when he turns his head, bearing about an inch of skin above his shoulders, around his neck. I hit him hard, with the side of my hand, and the one remaining rune I'd painted on my cheek burns white, then black, then red.

Hadrian crumples in a heap, all the light going out from his eyes. I break his fall as best as I can, grabbing him around the waist, but he pulls me down until I let him go, his head falling back against my knees.

He'll be alright, I tell myself, as I watch him dream. *I've used this spell a thousand times.* But its purpose, painted on my face for all to see, was my first lie of the night. *It'll protect us,* I'd told him, *if the ghost gets free.*

I don't know if he believed me, and now I'll never know. But either way, he trusted me, and that's always a mistake.

In the dying grass, stricken with the same illness that's killing the forest tree by tree, my friend shifts back to his human form, his clothes sagging to fit him. His feet are bare, his soles littered with scars, and the bracers on his arms smear with mud. Behind me, in my bow case, the ghost of the dead man I carry grows heavy again.

Working quickly, I strip off my quiver and pull the ancient wood from the leather tube, the curve of the bow once strung resembling a crescent moon. It's half the length of my body, silver and tough, like the willow tree I'd carved it from all those years ago.

You've grown attached, a voice says in my head, as I hold it. *I warned you not to do that.*

At my feet, I count Hadrian's breaths. They're steady and even, unlike my own.

"This is the last one," I tell the ghost in my bow, saying the words aloud just to spite him. And though he doesn't laugh or reply, I can sense his disapproval, his doubt, like a poison I've been forced to drink until I'm confident it can no longer hurt me. It still stings, but it's survivable, at least. "They deserve peace too."

From my satchel, I pull out the little vial with its little cork, the ghost inside thrumming against the glass. It's so delicate against the skin of my hand that I fool myself into thinking I could crush it if I tried. And it's cold; colder, even, than the harsh kiss of the wind, kicking up from under my cloak.

Ghosts can sense magic, too; they're drawn to the circles just as I am, sensing the nearest like a traveller drawn to the sound of a river or stream. Once free, they'll chase towards that source like it might take them somewhere they've been—or perhaps to some afterlife, if such a place exists.

I know so little about them, about this, but back when I was an apprentice ghost keeper, I was taught to lead those that linger in this plane from here to the next. I'd been taught to draw my own teleportation circles that lead somewhere, anywhere—no one really knows. The meaning of the runes have long been forgotten, and the destination they connect to is a place the living cannot go, even when we try. Only ghosts can disappear within.

I uncork the vial, watching as the tiny purple wisp slips out and expands, growing ever-brighter like the charcoal end of a match, burning in my hand like the sun.

The moment it's free, I drop the vial. I raise my bow.

At once, the ghost I've trapped in the bow roars to life, and I can see him standing next to me like he's there in the flesh. Broad in the shoulders and chest but tapered at the waist, like a dancer, with piercing red eyes, white hair, and dark skin, his form belies his power. Even in simple traveller's clothes, immune to both age and time, Elias is a force of nature, barely contained by the string in my hand.

Let me go, he says, and as I fire my first shot, he leaves me, exploding from the bow in a flurry of black feathers and black ash.

For all that Elias mocks Hadrian's fear of his powers, I know he relishes in it—in seeing what shifters today have become. He calls it *the breaking,* but by any other name he's a shifter too, fearsome and rabid, taking on the form of a large black crow with a wingspan so wide he could blow apart storms.

I used to hunt gods, he's told me, in the long mornings we've spent together, training beneath the trees, *in a different age of men. We are all made of bones.*

It's easy to believe him. Before me, Elias engulfs the entirety of the meadow like the grass itself is his shadow, every bend in every stalk his will, pushed down by the beat of his massive wings.

But in truth, he is no more powerful or alive than the ghosts he hunts, the ones I've untethered from their resting place in the rafters of that once-loved tavern. He's caught between the planes of life and death by the very magic he deems me unfit to wield, anchored to me and my silver bow like a sheep on a lead. He can only speak when I allow it, when I hold the bow in my hands; he can only strike when I allow it, with each arrow I loose. And he's forced to let me choose when and if he feasts. He can only guide my hand in his human form, gluttonous and greedy, and I choose this form often.

Elias, tied to the silver arrow I've shot into the night, soars through the air, his talons just missing the purple wisp as it curls upwards, bobbing in the wind. He screams, terrifying and raw, and I fire again. The chase is on.

The wisp dances higher, joyous and carefree, and I take aim, wondering if I knew them, as I always do. If this had been a friend, once, lost to the fire in that tavern, reduced to a name. I had been there on the day it burned, set the charge, fanned the flames, then dragged the bodies from the rubble; I'd checked their pockets, dug their graves. I'd been a different person then, though the result is the same.

Suddenly, the wisp takes off to the right, like a kite caught in a violent breeze. I fire a third arrow, then a fourth, and with each Elias races again and again across the meadow, his clawed feet and sharp beak snapping at the air.

I'm a murderer, in my own right, and I've accepted that—I've had to. I've sacrificed a hundred ghosts to that monstrous crow and never once hesitated, wracked with regret.

When the last arrow slips from my fingers, I watch as the wisp is cut through by the metal tip, then the shaft, then the feathers, before Elias consumes it whole.

The noise he makes is a wretched, horrid thing, like bones crunching and blood hitting stone. I can see the ghost dying in his hold, choking and spluttering just like every other before it, the colour fading away, but no one else is here to see the Elias that I know.

He'd offered me everything, once. He'd wanted to live. *I can make you powerful. I can reshape your world.* His pleas were what we'd expected, as apprentice ghost keepers; what we'd trained to ignore. None of us should have listened. None of us should have wanted to.

A master marksman, they'd called me, when I'd first enrolled at the academy. With Elias by my side, unseen, I could hit any target, moving or stationary, at seemingly any distance. *Marked by the gods for greatness.*

Using Elias like this, I've rebuilt every door my father's poor name and my mother's poor upbringing once destroyed. I win tournaments, impress kings. I'm a trophy to any rich man who can pay for the show, safe from the hallowed streets where my fellow apprentices once walked. I'm the only one left who knows of my life before this, drowning in discipline and broken skin. Elias ensured it.

At my feet, Hadrian suddenly stirs, and I remember I'll have to lie about what's happened. I drop down into the dirt beside him, careful to unstring my bow and hide it away, sealing Elias to his fate. His ravenous hunger is something I've contained—for now.

I tuck myself into Hadrian's side, feeling his body shift around me as consciousness returns to him, his skin growing fur, his feet growing claws. His bones seem to shake beneath my grasp, breaking and snapping to shift into something new. It's the only kind of magic I envy, though he trembles and whines from the agony of the change.

I watch his face—I always do. He's a young man under all that fur, with a nose that's broken in the middle by an awkward bump and cheeks marred by a half-inch of stubble I've grown to love. We contrast each other, he and I, his skin a burnished bronze where mine is pale, his hair the same golden yellow as his mane. The one thing we share is the colour of our eyes—dark green and opulent, like all mages this side of the mountain that divides our world—otherwise we'd have nothing in common at all.

Of course, when we'd first met, I'd been someone else entirely, wearing someone else's name and someone else's clothes. We'd been assigned the same academy dorm, the same stacked beds, the same shared bathing room, all marked with the same white runes. I hadn't had the power—or the strength—to change things back then. Now, I'm as much myself around him as I am around myself. He calls me *Pella*, like I've asked, and *girl*, like I've been both things all my life. And this truth—this one, precious truth I've chosen to share—has always felt safe with him. He's never once mocked the breadth of my arms or the flat plains of my chest, or the stocky, square shape of my face. He sees me, as I see him, even with the fur.

I close my eyes, waiting for him to find me in the grass. And when he does, the sounds he makes are small and choked, like we've both been struck down by bandits he was too slow to see.

I'll tell him another lie, when I open my eyes, taking in the worry on his face. Then I'll tell another, when I pretend to realize the ghost I've trapped is gone, and the rune paint wasted.

But for now, I'm safe here, in his arms. In the space between the heat of his hands and the earth, where I know in truth I should be buried, just like the monster I feed to win glory I have not earned.

WE FELLOW MONSTERS

MAWCE HANLIN

"You can still back out, you know. There's no shame in wanting to stay home."

When Dewey first asked to accompany him on this heist, Amrys denied him without hesitation. The younger boy had only just turned fourteen, and while this wasn't one of the more unsavory jobs Amrys was hired for, it was still leagues more dangerous than stealing food or picking pockets.

Unfortunately for Amrys, his little brother was just as stubborn as he was. He looked softer, with his long curls and his big amber eyes, but the boy's skull was about as hard as his horns were; once he got something in his mind, no one could talk him out of it. And while Dewey was crafty and smart, smarter than Amrys by far, despite being four years younger, that didn't mean he wouldn't worry.

"I can do it," Dewey insisted as he tugged his boots on. "You *know* I can."

"Just giving you an out if you need it." Amrys shrugged, tightening the strings of his binding stay until his breasts lay flat enough to be hidden beneath his robes. "Once we get there, we'll be too far to turn back, and I'm not opening another door if you get scared."

The younger boy huffed but didn't reply, grabbing the void bag

Amrys held out to him and slinging it over his shoulder. They only had two of them, each big enough on the inside to fit an entire household—or three—yet no larger than a messenger bag on the outside. Cas gave one to Amrys when he took his first job, his boss and benefactor assuring him the bag could carry anything he could grab. The second was given to them for this job specifically, layered with extra spells to keep the contents cooled and preserved if needed. Amrys kept that one for himself.

"Can we go now? *Please?*"

Amrys snorted and tugged his hood over his head, making sure it covered the curved nubs of his horns before moving to do the same for Dewey. The younger boy's horns were getting longer by the day, and unlike Amrys, he had no care to hide them or shave them down. He was lucky he didn't have a tail like Amrys did, since he doubted his little brother had the patience to keep it tucked away in his pants or behind his robes on jobs like this.

"Alright, brat, you remember the rules," Amrys reminded him. "Stay quiet, don't touch anything without your gloves, and if I tell you to do something, you do it. No questions. Got it?"

Dewey groaned, his hood sliding right back off as he dropped his head back in exasperation. "Rys, I'll be *fine*. We've run through this like fifty times!"

"And I know better than to assume you've listened all fifty times." Amrys raised an eyebrow, fighting back a smirk as Dewey tugged his hood back into place and flushed with embarrassment. "You're polished, Dewey. You may be good in the streets, but the home of an honestus is an entirely different monster. They're not just regular magic users like aedai are, they're *really* dangerous, okay? Now tell me you understand the rules, or you're not going."

"Fine, I understand. Can we *please* go now?"

Brat. Still, Amrys couldn't begrudge him his excitement. Despite the target, this was one of the easier jobs Cas had assigned him recently, and Dewey all but begged to be allowed to join. Amrys didn't like it—wishing he could keep his little brother out of the thief's life altogether—but he knew it was only a matter of time. Besides, two sets of hands were always more profitable than one.

"Alright. Keep your eyes open, use your aeda if you need it, and if I tell you to run, you run."

Amrys didn't wait for a response before waving a hand to open a door. The magic—or *aeda*, as was the technical term—in his veins leaping for the chance to act. The air shimmered for a moment and a puddle of black liquid began to seep from the floor, spiraling upwards before splitting open like a door to reveal a darkened forest rather than the dingy wall of their hideout.

He quickly ushered Dewey through and let it collapse behind them as soon as they passed, the dark aeda disappearing into the forest floor as if it'd never been there to begin with.

The lack of light from the hideout plunged them into darkness, and Dewey swallowed thickly beside him. Amused, he nudged his brother's arm and said, "stick close to me, okay? Rumor has it the honestus has a habit of collecting monsters. We don't want you getting eaten on your first job, do we?"

"*Monsters?*" Dewey's voice squeaked, and for a moment he looked like he might actually ask Amrys to open the door again and take him home.

Amrys grinned wide, his sharp teeth on display as he wiggled his fingers in Dewey's direction. The boy gulped, trying his best to put on a brave face. After only a moment of fear, however, Amrys snorted and nudged the boy forward. "Oh, don't be such a worry-wart. The only monsters he has are stuffed and mounted on his wall." That didn't mean there weren't plenty of beasts and critters in the woods that couldn't eat them just as well, but at least the woods were more familiar territory for them.

Lucky for them both, the honestus' mansion wasn't too far from where Amrys opened a door, so the journey through the woods was a short one.

The house itself sat pressed up against a cliff in the mountainside, the trees cut back just enough to leave a small clearing around it. It wasn't quite as large as Amrys would have expected for something Cas called a "mansion", but it certainly wasn't something he'd have expected to find out in the middle of the woods either. Too fancy with its big pillars and wide, coloured windows. A huge porch wrapped around the front half and there were more balconies than looked to be windows. For what little space it took up on the ground, it made up for in height, stretching up the side of the cliff so high it almost tilted, as if the mountain was the only thing holding it up.

Amrys dropped into a squat just inside the tree line, pointing up at the lit window at the very top. "Cas says the lab is at the very top of the house. My guess is there. Doors probably have extra protections, so the back windows are likely our best bet on getting in. Keep an eye out for traps though, okay?"

Dewey nodded where he crouched at his brother's side, worrying a leaf between his fingers and biting at his lip. "The light's on. What if he's home?"

"He's not." And if he was, Amrys would deal with it before Dewey had a chance to panic. Cas never specified if he wanted the guy alive or dead, and Amrys didn't care as long as they got what they came for in the end. "Boss says he's supposed to be at some fancy party in the city. It's in his honor, so he should be gone all night. He probably just left the light on, but still be careful, okay?"

Dewey didn't look convinced, but he didn't argue as Amrys pulled a dark veil of chaos from the forest floor and cloaked it over them, blending them into the night as they made their way across the clearing.

A quick peek through the window closest to the cliff face showed only a kitchen, and other than a small lock and an alarm staev carved into it, Amrys didn't see anything else to mark a trap.

He reached for the metal hoop hanging from his belt, thumbing through the various chains and trinkets that hung from it until he found a small silver cylinder containing his lock picks. Before he had a chance to pull them out, however, Dewey stopped him.

"Wait. Can—can I try?"

Armys paused, frowning. "You've been getting better, but I only have the one set—"

The boy shook his head and even in the cover of night, Amrys could see his cheeks flush. "I've, um . . . I've been practicing something. To help, I mean. I can open the lock faster and get rid of the alarm staev without your tools."

That was news. They didn't usually keep secrets from each other, especially not when it came to their aeda. But while he fidgeted with his sleeve, there was a confidence in Dewey's eyes that Amrys recognized.

"Alright," he said after a moment, gesturing to the lock. "Have at it, little brother."

Excitement broke over the kid's face, and he tore one of his gloves off with his teeth before confidently pressing a finger to the lock. No sooner had he touched it, did the metal corrode, silver fading to an ugly brown before the lock turned to dust, staev and all.

"Holy *shit*, Dew." Amrys ran a gloved finger through the dust left behind. "Where did you learn that?"

Dewey grinned, cheeks a ruddy red and chest puffed out in pride. "I just sped up its lifespan! I can only do it with small things right now, and it's harder with things that have magic in them, but I've been practicing on old iron bits outside the smithy's. You just make something decay *faster* and poof!"

"Alright!" Amrys smacked his shoulder, a giddy laugh bubbling up his throat as he grinned. "You'll be my secret weapon one day! Come on then, little reaper, in we go."

He helped to hoist Dewey through the window first before dropping in beside him, both of them pausing for a long moment to listen. When no alarms sounded or angry honestai came storming in, Amrys nudged Dewey aside and led him out the kitchen door.

The rest of the house was rather barren, all things considered. The sitting room just next to the kitchen had nothing more than a few chairs and a settee across from a blackened hearth. Books and strange stones lay scattered on a nearby table, and there were a few shelves further in with even more books shoved onto them. A set of stairs spiraled up the far side of the room, glass lanterns hung on the wall with little fireshards gathered at the bottom of them, waiting to be activated.

Dewey stepped away to reach for one of the nearest books, but Amrys grabbed his wrist before he could, shaking his head. "Top room first. That's our target. We can snatch anything else on our way back. We don't know how much time we have, so nothing out of arm's reach."

The younger boy pouted, but followed behind easily, taking Amrys at his word and only grabbing the few books he could reach on their way to the stairs.

As they made their way up, Amrys tapped the bottom of a few wall lanterns to open them, smirking when Dewey snatched the fireshards out of the air and shoved them into his bag. They weren't worth much, but they were incredibly useful and Amrys wouldn't mind planting a few around the hideout.

They bypassed floor after floor and room after room, each just as barren as the first aside from one or two near the top that looked cluttered with enough books to fill the university library in Caim. Amrys had to physically drag Dewey away from those floors for fear of losing the kid to the stacks.

By the time they made it to the top, Amrys was half convinced they'd climbed all the way to Nað, where the gods sat around ignoring what went on beneath them.

There were only two doors on the topmost floor, the lab with the door propped open and a chandelier of fireshards flickering from the ceiling, and another just across the way that remained dark and unassuming. Amrys made a mental note to check it later, just in case. If it was a storage room, he didn't want to risk missing something good.

"Draioct save us," Dewey breathed as they stepped into the lab and closed the door, "there's so much *stuff.*"

There really was. Where the rest of the house looked practically abandoned, this room was cluttered and overflowing. Jars of strange liquids and unusual body parts lined various shelves, books all but littered the floor, and the tables were all covered in potions and herbs and spell components.

The strangest things though were the monsters. Or rather, what Amrys assumed were monsters.

Stuffed beasts stood on pedestals throughout the room, some even mounted on the walls and hung from the ceiling. He recognized a scarce few, the rest entirely foreign to him.

A massive iridescent hound sat right inside the door, a gaping maw of glittering teeth poised to strike. A swarm of oddly shaped bat-like creatures with the tails of sand scorpions hung above a few of the nearby shelves. A wing of brown and golden feathers had been tacked to the wall above one of the work desks.

Worst of all though were the horns. A whole wall of them in the back of the room, each mounted on its own placard, all shapes and sizes and colours. He didn't know if they came from beasts or people, but just the sight of them had Amrys' own horns aching with a dull, distant pain.

He tugged his hood further over his head and took a deep breath, swallowing the rare nerves that threatened to overtake him. "Alright, grab anything you can, but prioritize ingredients and components, you're better with that stuff than I am. I'll focus on spelled items and the weird shit." Tearing his eyes away from the wall of horns, Amrys glanced at his equally shaken brother. "Cas wants anything he can sell to other honestai and merchants, so look for anything that has power or can assist in it. Move fast, but be careful and keep your gloves on. Dew?"

Dewey hadn't drawn his eyes away from the wall, his face pale and his hands clutching so tight at his satchel that his knuckles went white.

Amrys didn't blame him of course, but they also couldn't risk getting caught. *Especially* not if the crazy old man had a thing for horns.

"Dewey." He grabbed the kid's shoulder and turned him, bending down just enough to meet his eyes. "I need to know if you can do this. I know I said I wouldn't, but I'll open a door for you if you need to go home."

He almost preferred to. His own horns wouldn't do the honestus much good with how Amrys kept them shaved down, but Dewey's? They were beautiful, and Amrys would die before he let some ancient, kooked-up collector get his hands on them.

But his little brother was stubborn as they came, and Dewey shook his head, tightening his grip once more before releasing it. "I can do it. I'm fine. I can do it."

He didn't question him. Instead, Amrys just nodded and watched the boy take a deep breath and walk away, his gaze resolutely on the side wall rather than the back. Amrys only allowed himself a few moments of watching to make sure Dewey was okay before adjusting his own gloves and getting to work.

The room itself was fairly large, taking up what looked to be the majority of the top floor. Most of the space was taken up by the large ritual circle carved into the center of the room, the rest a clutter of shelves and crates and work desks. Even with the two of them, Amrys doubted they had any hope of actually making a dent in the room with the amount of time he was comfortable spending there.

While Amrys knew more about aeda itself than the magical items suffused with it, he'd learned over the years the kinds of things Casimir wanted him to look for. It was easy enough to parse through the shelves and grab what he could: bags of animal teeth, a mummified cat paw, a jar of beetle shaped buttons, basically anything weird that felt touched with magic.

They were about half-an-hour into work when Amrys heard it. He nearly didn't, hands deep in a box of jewelry as he was. The little gremlin inside him was practically dancing with delight at all the shining jewels and he eagerly dug into them, picking out whatever could fit his fingers and wrists and tail before shoving the rest in the bag at his side for his boss. But even the sound of the clinking jewelry couldn't hide the low rumbling hiss that vibrated through the floor and echoed in his bones.

His body froze instantly, muscles locked and heart pounding.

It sounded familiar in a way, though he was sure he'd never heard the sound before, and he followed it to a large covered shape just on the other side of the ritual circle. He reached for it, the strange hiss morphing into a series of rumbling clicks, each one a different resonance that sung in his sensitive ears. His fingers brushed the rough fabric and—

"Amrys! Amrys!"

The sound stopped, and his heart lurched in his throat as he whipped around to see Dewey careening toward him. The kid's arms were laden with books, a bubbling excitement lighting up his eyes as he bounced in place.

"Look what I found! He has all kinds of books on healing magic, and not just the Life aspect kind! Did you know Order aedai can also heal? And Time aedai? And he has a journal here that speculates *any* aspect would be able to, isn't that golden?"

This is why I don't bring you on jobs like this, Amrys groaned internally. Dewey was too smart for his own good, and he craved knowledge like an alcoholic craved a drink. It was useful, when Amrys had no idea what something said or if a book or scroll could prove important or not, but it also led to an easily distracted fourteen-year-old.

"Have you only been reading the books?"

Dewey's face screwed up with indignation. "No! I grabbed all the ingredients and components I could off the worktables and shelves! He even had a bunch of empty focuses in a drawer. Oh, and this!"

Balancing the stack of books with one unsteady hand, the boy pulled out a strange weapon from his bag. It was old, not well taken care of, but certainly unique with the metal shaped into claws and a dagger that folded within the curve of the palm. And while it didn't look like much, Amrys could feel a heavy power to it. Heavy enough to certainly interest their boss, at least.

"Besides," Dewey was still saying, "lots of rich aedai *love* books! So, I think it's fine. I did find this old journal with a lot of homemade recipes and stuff for healing tinctures, and I think I might keep that one for myself. It just doesn't seem like Casimir's thing, you know? And there's also—"

Click. Click. Clickssssss.

Dewey froze as soon as the noise started again, his eyes wide with fresh fear as they both turned back toward the cloth. "D-do you think it's a monster?"

Probably, Amrys didn't say.

The smart thing to do was ignore the sound and get back to work. Amrys knew better than to take risks on big jobs like this, but Draioct curse him, he was *curious*.

Before Dewey could stop him, he grabbed the cloth and gave a hard yank, the whole thing shifting and pooling on the floor to reveal what lay behind.

It was a cage. A massive one shaped like the little golden things rich women kept their songbirds in. The metal wasn't like any he'd ever seen before—dark and glistening like obsidian, but smoking like the doors he opened to travel.

Chaos. It was made of Chaos. As was, he suspected, the beast with the cage—the *monster*.

It was cat-like in shape—though its body looked stretched to accommodate an additional four legs—and about the size of a warhorse. It had a narrow head shaped like a fire bellow, and paws the size of a knight's shield. A tail *thwipped* behind it, the tip sharp and hardened, glistening gold to match the sharp tusks extending from its maw.

The whole thing dripped with a black, inky liquid that puddled on the ground beneath it before disappearing completely. Amrys could feel it—like a storm brewing beneath his skin, wind tugging at his limbs to draw him closer. He ached to reach out and sink his hands into the liquid, to know what it felt like between his fingers and in his pores.

"Amrys, don't—"

"You're not supposed to be in here."

Dewey shrieked at the new voice, the both of them whipping around to the now open door of the lab. Amrys clutched at the clawed blade Dewey found, flipping it open in case the old man had decided to come home early from the party, but there only stood another boy in the doorway. An *oniran* boy.

The boy had wide yellow eyes that looked too big for his face and slanted to a point at the inner corner, leading to a slightly crooked, hawkish nose. His skin was a golden-hued umber, a mane of charcoal curls piled atop his head. His ears, like most oniran Amrys had met, were long and pointed, though his looked almost fused with the skin as they followed the curve of his skull.

It was the wing though that drew Amrys' attention the most—a massive thing of browns and blacks and golds that drooped behind his shoulder and dragged across the floor. It didn't look very comfortable, just having the one wing. It pulled the boy's shoulder down a little and left him leaning more toward one side, the cane in his hand no doubt there to compensate for the weight.

Amrys never expected to find someone else like them so far from the Vein and the Rot. People further inland didn't tend to be affected as much by the Chaos plaguing Temenos, and yet there he was, just as different as Amrys and Dewey.

"Are you thieves?" The boy eyed the books in Dewey's arms and the bags on their hips. "Father doesn't allow others in his lab. You're going to get in trouble."

Father? Casimir hadn't said anything about a child, and while Amrys was prepared to kill an honestai if needed, he had strict rules against killing kids. He wasn't sure how old this boy was, but Amrys doubted he was any older than himself.

"Are you going to call for him? I don't want to fight you, but I'm not leaving empty-handed or getting caught, either," Amrys warned.

The boy frowned, head ticking to the side like a bird. "Why would I fight you?"

Amrys paused. "Because we're stealing from you?"

"You're stealing from my father," the boy clarified. "I have very few things for you to steal, but I suppose you're welcome to look if you like. I must insist you stay away from Blot, however, he doesn't much like people."

Blot? He named the thing?

The creature behind them growled low in the back of its throat, the liquid on its skin rippling with the sound.

"What happened to your wings?"

Draioct save us, my brother is an idiot. "Dewey," Amrys hissed, smacking the back of the boy's head. "Seriously?"

"What? I'm curious!"

The boy in the doorway hunched to make himself smaller, though he gave Dewey a small, shaky smile anyway. "I, um…it was removed. I'm okay now though, just can't fly away, is all."

Can't fly away, is all.

Amrys tensed at the wording, questions and observations clicking around in his head like tumblers in a lock.

The boy looked well fed, with a little fat on his cheeks and a healthy sheen to his skin. His brown and green robes were of nice quality and well taken care of. He looked ever the child of a rich honestai.

But there were smaller things that made something angry and protective itch under Amrys' skin. The way his clothes were well taken care of, but his wing feathers were ruffled and dull. The way his skin was healthy, but there were small bumps lining the edges near his hairline, scabbed over and inflamed. The way his fingertips were bandaged from where they peeked out beneath his robes.

What happened to your wings?

I um… it was removed.

His gaze traveled to the single wing hung over the first work desk, and the itching anger in his veins burst into a blazing fury.

"What's your name?"

Amrys shouldn't care, he knew that, but those tiny details added up and reminded him too much of his own past. Reminded him of his father's hands holding him down as his horn cracked and shattered against stone.

Can't fly away, is all.

Suddenly, his shaved horns weighed too heavy on his head.

"Um . . . it's Lorn?"

Amrys raised an eyebrow. "You don't sound so sure about that." Then again, they *were* strangers, so he couldn't blame the kid.

The boy's cheeks flushed darker, and he looked distinctly uncomfortable. "Well . . . it's the name my father gave me, I suppose."

More details. More reflections. Amrys tilted his head in consideration. "Is it what you want to be called, though?"

He'd caught the boy off guard, he could tell. His gold eyes widened, and he swallowed. "Um—I . . . " He shook his head. "I call myself Laeni. It's just—well, my father likes my boy name better. He says I'm a boy, so I have to have a boy name even though—well…I'm *not*."

Oh.

"Well, good thing he's not here, isn't it?" Amrys grinned wide at the kindred spirit across from him and shoved his hood down. His own curls were wild enough to hide the majority of his horns, but he knew Laeni noticed them immediately. "My father was more concerned about me being born with rotten blood than he was about me saying I'm a boy, but he's not here either. I'm Amrys, by the way, and this little monster is Dewey."

The boy groaned when Amrys tugged the tip of his horn, smacking his hand away. "It's nice to meet you! If you're not a boy, then are you a girl, or are you neither? I just want to make sure what to call you."

Laeni's lips popped open in a soft 'o', and even from this distance,

Amrys could see a distinct wetness to those golden eyes. After a long moment, Laeni swallowed and took a deep breath. "I'm a girl."

She said it with confidence, though she looked half surprised by it herself. Still, gender-crisis aside, Amrys knew they couldn't dawdle much. "Golden," he grinned again, tossing his arm over Dewey's shoulder. "How do you feel about coming with us? Can't promise it'll be as nice as a cushy manor and lots of fresh food, but you'd be free."

Dewey wiggled under Amrys' arm and all but bounced on his toes as he shoved his own hood off. "Oh yeah! Our house isn't as big as this one, or as nice, but we have the whole thing to ourselves! Rain gets in sometimes, but Amrys patched up the worst of the holes, so it's a lot better now!"

Laeni was still staring at them in surprise, her eyes darting back and forth between their horns and ears, like she wasn't quite sure what to make of them. "You're—rotten blood, you said? I thought—I mean, father just said I was born wrong. I didn't know—"

That there were others like me, he figured she wanted to say. If the guy wasn't an honestus, Amrys might have stuck around long enough to shove the weird clawed blade right through her father's throat and watch him suffocate on his own blood.

"You're not wrong!" Dewey stood up straight beneath Amrys' arms, raising his chin in stubborn defiance. "There are lots of people like us! And like, yeah, people don't usually like us, but that's *their* fault, not ours! And-and if you come back with us, we can protect you! Rys is really good at protecting me, so he can do the same for you! Right?"

Amber eyes turned up to him, but Amrys didn't need the begging to make his decision. He just nodded in agreement. "You'll have to help out and hold your own, but we've got the room, and it'd be damn safer than here."

She considered it, glancing back at the hall and then towards the large window. "I don't know how I could help, but—but I do not wish to stay here."

Good enough for me.

Amrys nodded decisively and checked the cracked timepiece hanging from his tool-ring. They might be pushing it, but he figured they could spare some time. "Alright then. Dew, go help her pack whatever she needs. I'll finish up in here. Make it fast, we've probably lingered too long as is and we need to get out of here as soon as we can. Meet me back in the kitchen in ten."

Laeni still looked a bit shell-shocked when Dewey bounded towards her and dragged her from the room, her cane tapping quietly on the ground. He'd have to make sure to account for that as well in his timetable.

Once they disappeared, he glanced back at the strange beast still prowling its cage and sighed. Something inside him panged at the sight of it, his Chaos calling out to the creatures. "Sorry, beastie. I can't risk taking two with us."

He got back to work instead of lingering on the aeda-colored eyes, not allowing himself anymore distractions as he snatched as many things as he could. He kept the strange dagger hanging from his belt just in case, though he hoped to be out of there long before anyone gave him the excuse to use it.

He'd only just checked his timepiece again—two minutes left before he had to make a dash for the kitchens—when the beast's growls and clicks began to fill the room once more. It thrashed against the bars of its cage, and the light from the fireshards above began to flicker. For a moment Amrys thought the beast was doing it, but there was no Chaos in the air to cause such a reaction, just a low veil of something else.

Shit—

Amrys whipped around the moment the ritual circle flared to life, the light so bright he had to shield his eyes to avoid the worst of it. Once the magic in the room died back down, he lowered his arm and met the beady black-brown eyes of the man now standing in the center of the room.

He didn't recognize the man, as Casimir didn't have any photos of him, but he didn't have to be Dewey-levels of genius to know it was the honestus that owned the home. Amrys could *feel* the power radiating off the guy, his aeda erratic and vertigo inducing the longer Amrys focused on him.

"You! Who let you in here? What are you—" Anger twisted the man's face like a foot wrinkling ironed fabric, his gaze flitting everywhere—the bag on Amrys' shoulder, the significantly less cluttered shelves, the clawed dagger on his hip—before landing on his still visible horns. He growled, the long sleeves of his robes beginning to flutter and billow as the air grew taut with magic. "A beast who dares to steal from me? I'll have your horns mounted on my wall, girl—"

Yeah, fuck that, Amrys sneered as he pressed his back against the uncovered cage, his fingers fumbling behind him for the lock. "Listen, I think there's been a misunderstanding. Why don't we just talk this out?"

"What have you stolen? What did you take?" The man took a step forward, only to freeze when a loud crash sounded downstairs. His eyes widened, a crazed sort of fury burning in them. "*Rats,* the lot of you. Always traveling in packs. How many of there are you?"

Amrys clutched the lock of the cage between his fingers and sucked in a deep breath as he felt the Chaos in the metal sinking into his skin. Like it craved him just as much as he craved it. "Well sir, there's a lot of things I've learned over the years, and one of them is that rats always know what the most dangerous thing in the room is. And sorry, but it's not you."

Before the man had a chance to respond, Amrys was moving. He grabbed the chaos in the lock with all his might and forced it to change, willing it into subjugation until it bent beneath him and reshaped into that of a metal ball. Without hesitation, Amrys lobbed the thing at the old man's head, crowing with delight when it smacked his forehead and sent him stumbling backwards.

And then Amrys ran.

He didn't bother to look back as he launched around the old man and sped towards the door. Even when the cage door slammed open with an echoing *clang* and the old man sputtered and cried out, he didn't slow down. Whether the old man was dead or not, Amrys wasn't sure, but he wasn't about to stick around and find out.

He sprinted down the stairs, and all but tossed himself over the railing when he was sure he wouldn't break something in the fall.

Dewey was wandering around the living room gathering books, his eyes frightened at the sight of his brother. "Rys! What's going on? What are you—"

"No time, gotta go!" Amrys' feet just barely touched the floor before he was moving again, snatching Dewey by the sleeve and dragging him into the kitchen where Laeni was waiting with wide eyes. "Your dad, does he have anti-travel wards?"

She jumped at the sudden question but nodded. "Yes. H-he doesn't allow anyone else here, so it's warded to just him."

Shit.

"Then we're running. We're running! Let's go!"

Neither kid argued with him as he kicked the back door open and shoved them both out. Laeni was slower than he liked with her awkward, uneven gait, but Dewey seemed to have expected something like that because he'd used some fancy looking scarf as a sling to tie her wing tight against her back to help re-center her. That, added with the cane, was enough to help her across the field and into the trees.

They didn't make it far into the woods before a loud snarl echoed around them and something slammed into Amrys' side. He tucked and rolled with it, ignoring his brother's cries. But instead of seeing the old man atop him as he expected, he was met with two dangerously sharp golden tusks only an inch away from his face.

"Amrys!"

"Don't!" He didn't dare take his eyes off the beast as he called out to Dewey, his heart throbbing so hard in his chest he was sure the gods could hear it. "Stay there! Don't move."

The fact that the beast hadn't already torn him apart was a good sign, he hoped, unless it enjoyed playing with its food. He doubted it, though. It just loomed over him, massive paws framing his body like the bars of its old cage, black chaos dripping from its skin before sinking into his own. It didn't have ears, but its head twitched to the side like it was listening for something.

Amrys' hands shook at his sides as he waited, heart in his throat and fingers itching for the clawed blade on his hip. He doubted he could get to it in time, but he wouldn't go down without trying.

Still . . . *I don't want to kill you*, he thought as he stared into those glistening eyes. *Please don't make me.*

A low rumble echoed from the beast, different from the clicks and hisses from before. Amrys held his breath as it leaned down, breath hot against his skin, only to freeze when it bent its head to his. Its Chaos brushed against the silver gem embedded in Amrys' forehead and sent a shiver down his spine, mingling with his own as if trying to calm him. It felt almost like…a thank you?

"You're welcome," Amrys breathed, a nugget of terror still crackling in his voice. "We monsters have to look out for each other, right?"

The beast gave one last push of its Chaos before standing. It glanced at where Amrys assumed Dewey and Laeni stood, bowing its head, and then it was gone.

"Holy shit."

"Rys! Oh my goodness, Rys! I thought it was going to eat you!" Dewey was at his side in the blink of an eye, grasping at his robes to search for injuries before wrapping his arms around the older boy's shoulders. "Oh gods, I thought—"

"Hey, hey, I'm okay." He hugged Dewey back, smiling at a shaken Laeni behind him. "I'm fine. It just wanted to thank me for letting it out. I only did it to cause a distraction., but I guess freedom is freedom, yeah?"

He met Laeni's eyes as he said it, a heavy question in the words. She knew what the beast's escape meant. Knew that her father was either dead, or incredibly injured, if his pet monster had made it out of the house unscathed. And while he wanted to help Laeni and give her somewhere safer to stay, he didn't want her resenting him for it along the way.

After a moment, a smile spread across her lips—pretty and wide and *free*—and she gave him a nod.

"Alright! Come on, you big softie, let me go." He pushed Dewey off and popped back on his feet, dusting the leaves and dirt from his robes. With a wave of his hand, Amrys opened another door of swirling chaos, revealing the dark interior of their hideout back home. Dewey didn't go far, clinging to his hand, and Amrys slung an arm over the gaping Laeni's shoulder.

"You're among fellow monsters now, and this is our den," he told her with a wide grin as he led her through the door. "Welcome home."

WHY?

AIMEE DONNELLAN

Consciousness is strange. It feels new, but there is no memory of what came before. First comes light, then sound, then an image. A face that is making the sound—the voice, the words.

"Hello!" it says. "I th-th—" There is a pause, and a breath. "I'll call you Char."

And so, they are Char, and this is their creator. A wizard, whatever that is. A woman, a she, whatever that means. She speaks with words, which Char cannot do—but Char's body is covered in small flames, and they can form them into shapes if they concentrate. She has two legs where Char has four, and only hair falling down from her head. She wears things over her body, fabric of different types depending on the day and what she calls 'the cold'.

Char is unclear of this concept of cold, and no matter the question marks they make, the wizard only shakes her head and assures Char it would be too tricky to explain.

"You are too hot," she says, gesturing to the flames that lick lazily across Char's fur. "I don't think you'll ever know cold."

Char learns about many things through her stories. Colours. The wizard is mostly blue, a pale shade for her face and a darker one for her hair. Somehow both are called blue, which seems confusing. Char prefers red, anyway.

The wizard can cast magic, using the little stick she likes to wave around, and then keep in the curl of one of her horns when she's not using it. She creates little fires a lot like the ones that come off Char's fur and tongue, and sometimes glittering lights in more colours than Char can yet name.

The rectangular things that line the walls are called books, and are the most important thing in the world. Char does their best to remember this, to remember everything. Food is their favourite thing to remember, so far.

They learn about small and big. The wizard is small, they think. She insists that she is more in the middle, that she only seems small because Char is big. Sizes are confusing.

But learning? Learning is good. It's not easy, but it creates an excitement in Char's chest that has their tail thumping until sparks shower all over the Char's special mat. The only problem with learning is when there is a question that Char does not know how to ask, when they have only the pictures they can make, and not the words the wizard uses. They do not know how to ask why they are not allowed to wander the tower as she does. (And if Char is Char, they do not know what she is. They have not worked out what picture could ask such a question.)

They try to be content with the instruction to stay on their bed and the mat that extends some of the way around the room from it. But their legs are beginning to ache and yearn for more. The mat is getting smaller and smaller as the days and nights pass, they are sure.

Sizes really are tricky.

One night, it is too much. Char must stretch their legs and explore or they may go mad.

They hop off the bed, down the mat, and halt. Ahead of them is the workbench with all the funny bits of metal and other shiny bits the creator works with. Beyond that, the books. Char has so many questions about the books, and what makes them so wonderful. Questions only their own investigation can answer, their own nose and paws and tongue.

Char leaves the mat. Steps onto the floor they have never touched before, the firm stone pressed against all the other large stones. So far, so good. Onto the bookshelf, then.

Many rectangles and colours sprawl before them, some high, some low. Some are thick, some are thin. All have the squiggles on the side that must mean something. Something about words. Certainly nice to look at. Char sniffs a few, long and deep. The scent is earthy and pleasant and makes their tail thump on the stone. So they lick the spines of the books closest to their nose, top to bottom with their long tongue.

Deep orange lingers on the spines after, fire leaving Char's essence and clinging to the books. Char blinks at how the fire spreads rapidly to the books next to them, and then the ones next to those.

Fire is good. Fire is warm, and comforting, and right. The colour is excellent too, bright in all the right ways. And how it dances! The creator had once talked of beauty, but with examples Char did not know or understand. Now Char sees it. The fire is beautiful.

A shout from nearby breaks the blazing reverie of it all.

"What—Char—*no!*"

The wizard's voice has never been like this before. Loud and piercing, hurting Char's ears. She appears next to Char, wrapped in her sleeping fabric instead of her working fabric, and the light of the fire reflects off her dark eyes.

Char, uncertain, makes a question mark out of flame above their head.

"You have to stay on the mat!" the wizard cries. "Th-th—you—get away, get away now, I have to-to—"

Her body shakes as her regular words fall away, and the rhythmic magical ones replace them. Her eyes flash with pure black, and dark magic gathers around her.

A new emotion seizes Char—one they will later learn is *fear*. A tightness in the chest, a screaming in their mind, a tug at their four legs demanding they *run run run*.

That's what had been said, wasn't it? *Get away. Get away now.*

Char sees the only way that might be *away* and bolts for the stairs. Down and down and down they go, around and around. They pass other rooms, things never seen before but mentioned, like the kitchen and the bedroom. Char still has no idea which is which.

The stairs come to an end and Char screeches to a stop, their claws digging into the wood, marring and igniting it simultaneously.

"Char!" comes a shout from upstairs. "Char, there's fire *everywhere*, fuck—"

Char does not yet know the word blame, but they feel its impact. Its implications. The fire is beautiful, to Char. To the wizard, it is not. But Char *is* fire. They cannot help how it is as much a part of them as their claws and size.

There is faint, soft light coming from the windows. The wizard says beyond the windows is *outside*. Char knows nothing of what awaits them there, but it is all that is left to them now.

One leap. A shattering of glass. Tiny pointy bits that barely scratch through thick fur.

And then, outside. It is dark and light and neither all at once, shadows all around just like in the tower but with twinkling lights above, so small. They are beautiful too, and Char wonders if they are tiny fires themselves, burning so sweet.

Crash!

It comes from the tower, with a shout that might be Char's name, and they are running again. Away, away, away. Just as she had demanded.

There are tall pointy things all around, with too many arms and no faces or legs, and they catch fire any time Char brushes past one.

They run and run and run. Is this the forest? The wizard had said something about being in a forest, but it's hard to make sense of. These tall things are so many, while the forest had seemed singular. Language is so tricky.

Char runs until the sky begins to change colour. It gets lighter, bit by bit, until colours paint the clouds. Char slows so that they might stop and stare up at them, wondering who had done the painting and how. Surely a large brush would be needed? But they had seen no such thing.

A glance behind them shows no sign of the wizard. There is only the forest, if that is what it is. No angry wizard. Nothing to fear, for now.

There is scarcely room for relief with how exhaustion tugs at every part of Char's body. They find a patch of dirt they can curl up on to sleep. The wizard's legs are much smaller than Char's—surely they have bought some time.

Sleep seizes Char immediately.

A small yelp rings through the air. It is enough to perk Char's ears, even in sleep.

When they crack an eye open, they see a small person, even smaller than the wizard. Different colour and proportions—skin and hair dark brown, the latter in bunches on top of their head.

"Woah. Big dog," the person says.

Char is not quite sure about the word 'dog' but does not dislike it. It is said with appreciation, and must be referring to Char.

They tilt their head and form a question mark with their flames.

The person points at Char. "You. You're a big fire dog."

Big and fire were things Char knew about themself already. But it does indeed seem that where the wizard and this little one are 'people', Char is 'dog'. Something about the word and the rightness of it makes their tail swish in the dirt.

Char creates an arrow pointing at their new acquaintance, then another question mark.

"I'm Tilly," says the person. "I'm a girl. Did you burn the trees?"

Char forms an image of the tall things they had been running through, and Tilly nods. Char mimics the motion as best they can.

"Did you mean to?"

Char hesitates.

"Do this for yes," Tilly says, nodding again. "And this for no." She rotates her face from side to side. "Got it?"

Char does the nod.

"So, did you mean to burn the trees?"

Char moves their head from side to side in the movement for no.

"It just happens?"

Another nod.

"Where do you live?"

Char is not sure how to convey that they do not know. That the place that had been home no longer is. All they can do is hang their head and make a soft noise of uncertainty.

Tilly's eyes widen. "Oh no. Maybe you can come home with me!" She frowns a moment later. "Oh. But you might light things on fire. I can see how that might happen by accident. Is it just your feet?"

Char forces out a cough that showers sparks across the dirt. Tilly jumps in surprise, her eyes lighting up for a moment before a frown settles across her brow instead. Her hands rest on her hips.

"Maybe I could find you some special shoes. And you could practice coughing into your elbow—that's what Mum says I have to do, anyway. If you . . . have an elbow."

The two compare limbs, in search of Char's elbow, and do not find one. Tilly is certain, however, that Char could cough into where their front leg meets their body.

"Come with me, a bit closer to home," Tilly says. "I'll see if I can find something fireproof for your feet!"

They walk a while, Char having to go quite slowly since they are about three times Tilly's size and naturally move much faster. Tilly keeps some distance from Char, claiming that Char is very hot and will burn her if they get too close.

Char is not sure what burning means, or why it is bad, and creates a question mark.

"It happens to a lot of things that aren't fire dogs when we get too close to fire," Tilly explains. "It hurts a lot. Sometimes things go red or black until they get better. Trees don't always get better, though. They're not as good at fixing themselves as people."

Char wonders if the books can fix themselves as well, back in the tower, or if they are more like trees. They create the shape of books, then a question mark.

Tilly shakes her head. "Fire is super bad for books. Books can take a lot to make. The fire will burn away all the pages and the words."

The wizard's upset makes more sense now. The books that Char had touched, just wanting to see, are perhaps forever ruined. And the books had been the wizard's favourite thing in the world. No wonder she had wanted Char gone.

Char paws at the dirt and whines in their throat as the memories play over and over, worse each time they repeat. It had been an accident. They truly hadn't known what their fire would do. And now, they know nothing but the tower and the trees and Tilly.

"You're sad," Tilly says.

Char nods, the up and down that means yes.

"I wish I could give you a hug. But I'd get hurt." Tilly gives them a smile. "It's okay, though. I'll be your friend."

Their tail wags with such vigor that the thump it makes against the ground is enough to make Tilly jump. She giggles.

"Shhh. I'll need to hide you. Mum says I can't have a dog until I remember to water the flowers, and I keep forgetting. And you're big and tricky to hide."

They stop at a gap between some trees that Tilly evaluates with a deep crinkle of her forehead. Finally, she nods, and asks Char to lie down and get comfortable. While Char does this, she tugs at some of the surrounding branches and shrubbery to put more barriers between Char and the view from town.

"I'll be back soon," she promises once she's done, and hurries off.

Char waits. It isn't an unpleasant thing. The wind moves through the trees like a song, and there are fascinating bugs in the dirt. Char cannot chase them, since they might start another fire if they do not stay put, but it is exciting to watch the bugs scuttle about, nonetheless.

The sun has shifted in the sky by the time Tilly returns. She even has snacks—bits of dried meat that Char gobbles up as soon as they are thrown.

Char's flames create a smiling face like Tilly's own to convey their gratitude. The girl beams.

"Yummy?"

Char nods and finishes up all of the offerings before stopping for breath.

"Wow, you ate that quick," Tilly says with a small frown. She taps her chin with her finger. "I guess you need a lot of food, like a horse.

Or… even more than a horse. I'll figure it out! Or can you catch your own food? Like rabbits or something?"

Char makes an image of a rabbit in their head flames to check they have the correct creature associated with the word, and Tilly nods. Char has never tried to eat a rabbit, but they could certainly try it if Tilly thinks it's a good idea.

They *had* seen a few of the hopping creatures in the forest, but they had scampered away at the sight of Char, giving nothing but a view of their bouncing fluffy bottoms and tail. Investigating may involve trying to go much more slowly and quietly.

"Where did you come from, anyway?" Tilly asks. "What did you eat there?"

Char creates an image of the tower, and Tilly's eyes grow wide.

"The wizard? She's meant to be so powerful. But they say she doesn't like us, that she stays up in her tower because she doesn't want to talk to anyone, so we can't go see her."

Char understands the concept of like, but had not given the idea of *not* liking something much thought. They've not exactly had the time to consider such things. There are a few things that the wizard had complained about from time to time—the texture of cold eggs, how some people folded the corners of book pages, and the fact that certain flowers made her sneeze.

They can only make a question mark. Why would the wizard not like Tilly or her village?

"I don't know. Some people just focus too much on what they don't like, and not enough on what they do," Tilly says. "Sometimes they just don't have enough love in their hearts."

Char remembers the sound of their name billowing down the stairs of the tower, remembers *get away, get away, get away.* They hang their head. It would seem that the wizard does not like them either.

Tilly sits down in front of Char, gives them a small smile, and begins telling them a story about the farmer and some scarecrows in a field who were not actually scarecrows. Char is immediately riveted.

Tilly talks for hours, until the sky is beginning to darken.

"Mum will be looking for me soon," she says as she gets to her feet.

"I'll be back tomorrow. I'll bring food, but you might need to go look for rabbits. If you're gone when I get here, I'll wait."

Char makes the image of the moon to bid her farewell. Tilly stops and smiles again.

"I'm really glad we met. I think we both needed a friend."

Char nods, watches her go, and settles into the dirt to get some early rest. It's been an odd day, but there is a new glow in their chest. A new kind of warmth. Nothing to do with fire, nothing at all. Is it love? The thing that ought to be in people's hearts?

Tilly had said that love is what is supposed to be there, and only something that is supposed to be there could feel this good, so it must be.

Love feels good. Having a friend feels good.

The sunrise arrives before Tilly does the next morning, so Char carefully leaves their hideaway in search of rabbits. It is impossible to catch rabbits without colliding with and igniting a few trees, but the rabbits are tasty and go a lot further than the small bits of food Tilly had managed to grab yesterday.

Char heads back to the hideaway, belly full and content, and finds Tilly waiting.

"Did you find any rabbits?" she asks.

Char nods and licks their lips at the memory. Tilly giggles.

"Good job! I brought some other snacks just in case." She throws little blue sweet things that burst in Char's mouth in a shower of sensations that makes them shake their head in surprise. "They're blueberries! What do you think?"

Char has no idea. Comparing them to rabbits seems absurd, but they are tasty to gobble up and Char wastes no time doing so.

"Do you want to hear about the time a dragon flew over the village?" Tilly asks.

Char nods, and Tilly spins as many stories about her home and the people there as she can, for hours and hours. Char is starting to know the people of the village without having ever seen them—knows the butcher has a large orange moustache and a funny hat, but is not clear on what a moustache actually is. There's a lady with large arms in the forge—a

very hot place that Tilly thinks Char would like but perhaps not fit inside
—the lady sometimes lets Tilly hold a hammer just to see how heavy it is.
Tilly's mother works hard selling bread and cakes and has Tilly help her
in the mornings when she has to get things ready for the ovens.

"I have to go earlier today," Tilly says. "Mum wants help with some
new recipes she wants to try before tomorrow. Will you be alright?"

Char has little reference for these things, but they nod in a firm
belief that they will be content to muse on the many things she has told
them about. Char does not know many people, but the theory of people
is starting to make a bit more sense.

The next day, though, Tilly asks a trickier question.

"If you came from the tower, did you know the wizard?"

Char stops gnawing on a leg bone she brought them as a treat, and
nods before continuing to chew.

"Where did you come from before that?"

Char shakes their head, making a question mark at the same time.
They are not sure they were ever anywhere before that. If they were,
they certainly don't remember.

"Oh. You're not sure?" Tilly frowns. "Did you leave because the
wizard wasn't nice?"

Char has no idea how to convey what happened. They try to make
images of books burning, of the wizard shouting, of how their feet are
racing down the steps. It's difficult; they do not usually make images so
lifelike or moving. Tilly's eyes go wide, the brown of them igniting with
the bright reflection of Char's flames.

"Oh," Tilly says. "I'm sorry. Well, you have me now. Everything will
be okay."

That night, after Tilly's departure, a rumble rips through Char's
stomach. It demands more than the bread rolls it had been brought that
day. It needs a proper little hunt for food—rabbits or something similar.

Char creeps back to the forest. It feels good to hunt again, even if
the rabbits are trickier to find this time around. There are also some
birds in the trees, fascinating things that Char can recognise vaguely
from when they would visit the tower's windows. They are looking
especially tasty now. The branch is not so far that Char couldn't reach it
with one excellent jump.

Char runs, leaps, and snatches the owl in their teeth as they collide with the rest of the tree, snapping the branch and falling into the tree behind it as well. Flames kick up fast around them. They begin to lick at other nearby branches, closer together than where Char had hunted before. They should have noticed it, the trees being more dense here. But they had been so hungry that they had wandered a different way in search of rabbits.

The fire spreads, and spreads, like with the books in the tower.

The light is bright and beautiful, and Char is stuck watching it with awe. It feels like home, like closer to home than anything they have known yet. Surrounded by an inferno, by everything that feels like them, not trying to suppress their own nature.

They cannot help the delighted howl that escapes them. They dance in the fire and laugh at how it tickles them.

It is hard to say what time passes. They cannot see the sky for the blazing of the fire that lights the forest.

But then there are shouts.

Char whirls around and sees people—fully grown ones, with large sticks and some other things Char does not recognise. The people are gathered outside the fire, looking in.

"Gods, look at the size of it," one of them says to another.

"We're never going to get the fire under control," a different one says. "It's coming so close to the village."

Char whines; the village will not mix well with fire. The people there will get hurt. This isn't what Char intended at all.

A note of exclamation forms in Char's flames, but the people do not seem to see it. Char wishes they could do more than bark and whine, wishes they could say the word *sorry*, wishes their mouth could form it like a person can. They try anyway, and it is just noise.

"Stay back, monster!" one of the people shouts.

Char recoils, and a crossbow bolt flies past their shoulder.

"Uncle Trev, no!"

Tilly. Char can see the shape of her, running to the side of the one who had loosed the bolt, tugging on his clothes desperately.

"Tilly, go home! Now!"

Tilly turns to Char. "What happened? There's too much fire. It's going to hurt the village. Why did you come this way? The trees are too close together."

How to convey it was an accident? Char can only shake their head. They don't know what image would help.

"Tilly, the fire is too much, go *home!*"

Tilly's eyes blink, filling with water. "I thought we were friends. I thought you knew the fire would hurt people. I thought you knew you had to be careful."

With a disappointed final glance, Tilly turns away and walks until she is out of sight. Char barks after her in protest, and another crossbow bolt flies. It grazes past Char's leg this time, and fear returns with its cold claws gripping Char's chest as they yelp and turn to run.

For the second time, Char flees the sound of shouts and the crackle of flame they have created. They fly across the ground, away, away, away. Their paws thud against the ground with each great stride and it matches, it is all *away, away, away,* and *no, no, no* and *sorry, sorry, sorry.*

They run until the sky changes colour, and then, to be safe, run even further until their feet ache and they can only come to a stop.

Wherever they are now, it is a place with no trees. There are only patches of grass with mud covering them, leading the way to the largest body of water that Char has ever seen.

They are not sure what they think of water, so they collapse into the mud and watch the ripples, and how they reflect the sunlight. That seems beautiful too. Beautiful like the wind in the trees, like the dance of flames, like the way Tilly had laughed and smiled.

If there is so much beauty in the world, in nature and in the people, then why does no one think that Char is beautiful? Why are the things that feel the most right to Char the ones that lead to shouting and fear and anger from everyone else?

One of them had called Char a monster. Char does not know much of monsters—are they creatures who are not beautiful? Creatures who can only hurt others?

A whine leaves Char's muzzle as they bury it in their paws. That is not a good thought. Char didn't ask to be the way they are, so alive with fire that wants to jump and greet everything they touch. It would certainly be easier to be less fiery, but that is not how Char is. And would they be Char at all, if they did not feel that leap in their chest when they see the fire, when they dance in it?

Char stays there for a long time. Or at least, it feels like a long time. The light on the water shifts as the day changes, and it mesmerises Char almost enough to ease some of the pain.

That's what it is, pain. Pain like when they had tripped over their own paws and hit hard floor, but pain that is in their chest. Char wishes they knew how to make it go away. There is no one here now to cast a healing spell.

The sun starts to go down, and the colours spread over the clouds again, continuing to show that there is so much beauty everywhere. Surely Char has only seen some of what the world has to offer? But where could they go, where people would not be upset with them? Where they would not be a monster?

"Char—"

Only one person knows Char's name. Char whirls around, almost tripping on their paws like when they had been smaller.

The wizard stands there. Her long hair is a waterfall of knotted dark blue, her robes covered in grime and soot.

Char braces themself closer to the ground and growls. They form a question mark above their head. Why is she here? Why did she make Char like this? Why? Why? Why?

"Oh, Char," she breathes, and her eyes get that same water that Tilly's had. "I'm so sorry."

Char is confused. They stay put. They form another question mark, then burning books, then burning trees. They try something trickier, her hands holding a smaller version of them—then another question mark.

Several moments pass. The wizard's eyebrow furrows over her intense, watery eyes.

"Why did I make you like t-t—like how you are?" She sighs and steps closer, bit by bit. "To be honest? I didn't. You were supposed to be a regular dog, Char, just one made of magic. But every magic has a source. The one I used t-to power the spell was more rooted in fire than I t-t—expected. So you… came out like this."

Char repeats their question. Her creation of them. And a question mark.

"Why did I make you?" Her body shakes, in a way Char somehow understands, the emotions in her trying to burst out. "Char, I—I just wanted a friend. People can be t-tricky, and judgemental, and I always seem to say the wrong thing. I used to have someone with me, someone I loved *so* much, but she left. And I was so alone in the t-t—" She stops, as she sometimes needs to when the words get stuck on her tongue, and takes a deep breath. "Back there. I wanted a friend *so* badly. So I made one."

Char makes a burning book image again. Then one of her, shouting.

The wizard nods, through her tears, and steps closer again until she is as close as Tilly ever got. "I'm so sorry," she says. "I should never have shouted at you. I know you didn't mean to. I was so upset, but I never wanted you to leave. I didn't realise what I'd said until — I just meant to get away from the books. Not me. But you couldn't have known, you were too new. I'm so, so sorry."

Char can only stare. They play their memories back, with this new knowledge, to see if it fits. They are no expert on people's emotions and words. It could be as she says, that she had never intended the hurt caused.

The shine of tears in her eyes, the gleaming darkness of them where everything else is so blue, speaks to Char's heart.

They believe her. It comes as a rush of warmth where the world had been starting to be utterly absent of it. Someone knows of them, of their igniting nature. She is here, apologising for her own actions instead of condemning Char's.

Char can only think to form the shape of a heart—which Tilly had said can represent love—and then a question mark.

"Yes," the wizard says immediately, fiercely, somehow speaking the words from deep in her chest in a way Char can *feel*. "I do love you, Char. You're my dog. My friend. And I promise, I'll make a new tower. One where the books are safe, or immune to fire somehow. One where you have the freedom to do anything you want. I should have had that from the start, when you came to being as you did. You're beautiful. I could never wish you different."

Beautiful. She had called them beautiful.

All at once, the day is everything that Char could have wished. And it is too much. They drop their head into their paws again, their body shuddering just like hers, every emotion bombarding them worse than any crossbow bolt.

The wizard waits. She sits, and they sit in a silence of mutual understanding, of two beings who feel so apart from most. It is unexpected, and it is everything.

She talks and asks of Char's travels. Char asks about sunsets and lakes and light reflections, and somehow she understands yet again, even just from the images.

"We'll need a lot of interesting materials for our new home," the wizard muses. "And we can pick a new location. Should we go on an adventure, first? Don't worry, I have spells that will keep things safe."

Char tilts their head. The wizard murmurs something and her hand pulses with the dark colour of her magic before spreading over her body. She reaches the hand out and touches Char's fur, running her fingers through it. There is no burning, no pain, no flinch. Only a smile.

Char's leg goes wild, thumping against the ground in tandem with their tail. The wizard giggles.

And that is how Char learns about hugs and looks forward to an adventure full of them.

ATLAS
BEAU VAN DALEN

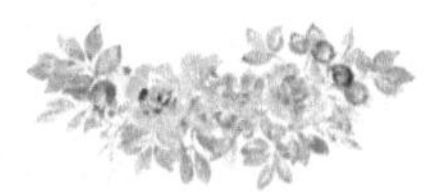

Today you asked me why I would rather be a monster than myself.

There is blood in the ocean, and I am both the water and the one who is bleeding. I am old. I've been sick. The pain that erodes my mind is worse than the hurt in my joints. Every day, I am fire, burning to light up a world that won't ever welcome me with grace. I waited, a year, then two, then sixty, and time had passed, and I was stuck—it feels as though life has not begun yet. My life as a man. My body a costume sewn into the role of a good wife, a perfect actress admired by all, my reality falls over nobody's ears.

Known to none, I wander.

I wander, because there is nothing left to do.

I wander, because I heard the rumors long ago, spoken from the mouth of a local fortune-teller.

If I walk through the woods long enough, I will get there.

Where there *is, I haven't the slightest clue, but it is better than waiting—watching, as life passes me by.*

There is a light, and then a ringing in the air that cools even though we are in the middle of summer, and the pine trees should be hot and my skin a sweltering warmth. Still, I find myself shivering.

The light wades between two branches before it disappears. I run. Towards it. A bright orange glow. A firefly in the dusklight.

My only way home.

"Home?" I speak the word aloud, like a foreign language on the tongue. It is strange. I do not think of my house, nor my husband, nor my work when I say the word for what feels like the first time.

I think of the forest and what lies ahead. Veinlike patches that glow in the darkness. Shadows that call out to me. A cavernous disappearance.

The grotto looks inconspicuous when I arrive before its eye, yet I know it is *something more*. I have wasted away in this town for decades; I have never once seen it. I could not have missed it. It was not here last night.

When an owl hoots into the distance, I am compelled to stride closer to the ravenous blackness. The air is not as cold as it was before. The tangerine orb that led me here has long-since faded, replaced by a full moon in the sky—everything would be normal if not for the cave.

Around my lone figure, the trees sway in the wind as if dancing, whispering secrets amongst themselves that only they will ever know.

I have a feeling that if I walk away now, I will never see this place again.

However, something in my heart tells me that if I enter the grotto, my life as I know it will wilt into a fragment of the past, and what I am today will cease to exist.

I take a step forward.

I don't look back.

And time reverses.

I am young again.

But something has changed.

Today you asked me why I would rather be a monster than myself.

I thought I would find an answer by coming here; however, I'm still looking.

The world is without color in the selenite caves. That is why we must populate it with love—shades of ourselves—in order to survive.

I have adapted to life well enough to survive here. It is almost as if the descent I'd made long ago deep into these caves never occurred. I can barely recall what it felt like for my body to reshape itself into what I am today: neither man nor woman, a being destined to never be gazed upon by the eyes of another, I have settled for sedation over joy.

I must never show my face at the surface again. This was the term which I agreed to when I first sought refuge inside the grotto. Living in this body does not feel right, but it is better than the last. For once, I am not in the spotlight. I do not run the risk of being shunned by society for being myself, we all found our ways down here for a reason: we did not belong.

So why does my heart still feel empty?

Why can't I be happy?

Amid a crowd of lively spirits whose skins glow iridescent shades connected to mine, I squeeze through bodies that feel both too cold and warm to be alive, until I reach a rockbound clearing where food stalls have been installed beside an underground lake. I stride through monster-made alleyways that seem to bend and curve a little more with each passing step, and once I reach the end—the place that serves my favorite meals—I take the first seat I see and order a Plate of Memories. I devour gold globes, mixed inside sticky sweet goo that leaves tendrils of what looks like honey, yet is magic that links me to the past. The liquid slips past my tongue in an effortless motion.

I swallow it all, monster that I am. One gulp. And it is gone.

The other stalls may be able to offer emotions, the wildest possible tastes in the world, but nothing surpasses reliving my favorite moments from life as a human. It keeps me tied to the person from whom this shell was created from, I try and *want* to honor that person daily, whenever I can. Without light, without the sun and the moon representing the passing days, without a sky, it is too easy to forget.

Where I come from.

Who I am.

Silly, isn't it? I think to myself. *Considering I came here to forget. To be something else.*

The truth is that, sometimes, I yearn for something more. It isn't that I wished to roam the depths of this darkness for eternity—I did not want to lose myself, but I could not stand to live the way that I was, with the idea of dying the way that I was in mind. *If I cannot be a man, then I will be a monster, and I will wear my secrets across my body as scars that have been turned inside out,* I thought, and I still believe that. My deepest fears and pains hung out like laundry for all to see, that is what made me, that is who I am today.

There are no mirrors in the selenite caves. Maybe that is for the best. I would rather not see what sort of shape I've taken that causes every monster I meet to run far. Although I can imagine it, since most of them look alike—tall, gruesome, wide and mostly made of stone— their eyes always widen in a way that scare me when our paths cross.

Once again, I do not fit in.

Another year passes. And another. And another. Time melts into itself, a hotpot of past-present-future, *and—what year is it now?* I have lost track of it all. This feeling finds me wandering again, farther than the food stalls, the monsters and their shadows. I arrive at a tent that I cannot recall ever seeing before. The moment is like the memory I sometimes eat for dessert: one in the nighttime where everything changed, and the grotto that should not have presented itself before my eyes did.

Scratch marks cover the tent. I take a closer look and find that inside those marks reside the universe, constellations of many kinds. I cannot resist the pull of this place. It draws me in. I am inside before I know it. A misshapen monster stands behind a table, observing me with evergreen eyes. I recognize her. I do not know why I do. But I know that she is the fortune teller from long ago. Something about her mannerisms, her state of being, tells me it is the woman I met many moons ago.

But I don't acknowledge it. I don't even have time to. Before neither she nor I can utter a breath, the fortuneteller drops a lantern that lands with a clank across the makeshift stone table separating us. She rises to her feet. Floats toward me, turns into the night sky I was so fond of and missed dearly.

She holds my hand, then disappears. When I open my palm that had tightened into a fist, there is light that emanates out of the callouses on my fingers. She has shared knowledge with me, that is clear, because thoughts that are not mine flood my mind: *You may leave this place, as long as the lantern is lit—however, abandon it or let its fire run out, and you will not be welcomed back.*

When I grab the lantern, the tent recedes into oblivion until it is gone. If it weren't for the weight of the fortuneteller's gift inside my palm, I'd think this were a dream.

Leave? I ponder on the possibility as I stare down at a hollow dip, protected inside glass, where a fire can be lit. *Will this truly allow me to explore the surface? And*—my eyes widen—*how would that work exactly?*

I don't like that I am curious.

I try to push the thoughts away. Yet, once whispers fade after every monster is done partying, dancing until late into our version of the night: I grab the lantern. I light its candle that looks to be made of selenite, and although it should not be possible, it takes fire and burns.

Nobody notices when I slip away. They are all asleep, lost deep inside a collective dream.

It has been so long, even so, I have no trouble finding the exit. *The way out.* It is as though my legs know where to take me and I am just here, along for the ride.

The closer I near to the surface, the brighter it all gets. The caves are alive, in a process of constant metamorphosis that crashes down across its walls, invisible waves of celestial glitter—I see it all. *I see it all.* Ceilings home to lustrous selenite glowing pale white, doused in rainbow reflections from the scales and gems across every monster's back. *I see it all.* Pitch darkness, then—violet hues from the waking of dawn, which tint the cavern walls in splats of pastel light.

When I first entered these caves, night had fallen. It was quiet out here. I could not see a thing. To be met with the sight of morning again, everything drenched in the colors of the world after so long, it feels as though I've woken from one of the longest dreams.

I step out of the grotto; it is covered in plants now, little insects and life.

I squint at the horizon.

I might not have aged, but the world has.

The lantern sways in the wind, creaking, as I observe the forest trees —the same ones that had bidden me farewell as I was spat out of one world, then thrown into another. The trees have grown taller, too. I can barely see the sky now; it is all covered in fresh pine. The house I used to live in has disappeared. There is birdsong in the air.

It is peaceful—until it is not.

The sound of a bucket being knocked over, water sloshing and pouring out onto grass, catches my attention. I turn my head towards it. I find myself facing a well—one whose presence I cannot recall being here either, the last time I inhabited the surface. The bucket is still here, in all its wet wood and dangling steel-black handle glory, but its owner is gone. Hurried footsteps that crunch against leaves in the distance is the only proof that anyone was ever here.

Panic rises in my throat and lodges itself there. *Someone has seen me.* I take a step back and sink into damp soil that gives under my weight. *Someone has seen me.* Yet, when I peer down at myself, the hands of a monster are nowhere in sight. They are human hands. Human feet. Human legs and, *oh*—

Whoever that person was, they likely did not run away because of my unsightly appearance, I think… They ran away because I am naked. "But how?" I ask the question aloud, hearing the deep rumble of my voice, like I had always envisioned it.

How?

I almost release the lantern out of utter joy. I am ecstatic. I want to jump around the forest, to kiss the trees and sing at the clouds, for I have been given a second chance. I am young.

I am the man I've always wanted to be.

Finally.

Finally.

I stay outside beside the grotto until the candlelight threatens to run out. I don't want to go, but I also don't know what will become of me should I stay. The fire is on the verge of dimming. The selenite has almost burned through entirely; if I'm unable to replace it, at least, I'll be able to relive the memory of this morning every day. I would gladly settle for that—one day of being me. Where nothing feels wrong, and I do not carry the weight of a body that feels foreign on my shoulders.

Before I leave, I pick up the now-emptied bucket. I fill it with water and leave it on the well's ledge. When I catch a glimpse of my reflection, my heart skips a beat. A tear rises to my eye as I touch my face. My voice trembles when it leaves my throat.

"It's me."

I bid my farewells to the forest as I delve back into the cave, where my body warps again into that of a monster's—but I know that I am inside this shell now. I don't need to see it twice to know. Even if nobody can see it: *I'm here.*

"I'm here."

Today you asked me why I would rather be a monster than myself.

Yet, being a monster does not mean what I thought it did before.

I wake to the sight of the lantern intact. The selenite candle inside has regenerated overnight. My pulse rises to my ears, and heat to my face, I am not hungry for memories anymore. I want to go outside.

I want to experience life through my eyes; not inside a stuffy stall, where the warmth of the food is overbearing sometimes and I cannot breathe. For the first time in years, I eat something with savor; I look forward to the day ahead. Once my stomach is full, and my heart craving another venture to the surface, I set the lantern's candle ablaze.

I set off, away from everyone else. My steps impatient, *I cannot wait to leave.*

Maybe I'll get there and still look like the monster I am today.

Maybe I'll never see my reflection again.

Still, I want to taste the freedom I relished in yesterday. I have a feeling it'll happen once more.

The journey is not as tiring as it was before. As I set foot across a land I used to loathe yet cannot get enough of now, I transform. I am Me again.

I'm not alone, though. I realize it when a gasp makes itself known throughout the morning's gentle silence. Long white gown swaying in the breeze, curly red hair hides a blush of freckles across the face of a woman by the well, who holds the same bucket as the one I came across yesterday. Her celeste eyes that lean into opal remind me of what the gems on my skin reflect across selenite when I am a monster.

She is on the verge of leaving when I call out to her, raise my arm and yell, "Wait!"

The woman turns around. She gives me the side-eye as she hugs her bucket closer to her chest. Her arms are trembling. "And why on Earth should I listen to a man who spends his days parading naked in the woods?"

"I—" My lip twitches. I reach for her, but I eventually close my fist and let my arm drop back down to my side. Because she has a point. "I lost all my clothes." It's not a total lie. They were ripped to pieces when I became one monster out of many who roam the selenite caves. "I can't get new ones"—I motion toward my body— "in this state."

The woman averts her gaze. She huffs, a faint dusting of pink flushes her cheeks. "Wait here."

Before I have a chance at replying, she is gone.

I wait for what may have felt like forever to any ordinary person but, to me—someone who truly knows what *forever* feels like—the moments I spend awaiting her return are barely a ripple in time.

I am surprised when she comes back, though.

"What?" she asks, as she throws a pile of clothes my way.

I go through the fabrics, slipping into trousers, a shirt and some shoes. I didn't expect her to give me this much. "You believe me," I say.

She scoffs, crosses her arms whilst she taps her foot against the soil. "I can always tell when someone is lying."

I would question it, however, considering I come from a magical cave, I don't think her statement is that unreasonable. "Thank you."

There is a moment of silence in which neither of us speak another word. I almost expect her to leave.

But instead, she comes closer. She tilts her head to better look at me and holds out a hand to touch my face, as if she wants to make sure that I am not a ghost, something elusive or intangible.

Her touch is warm. I lean into it on instinct. I gulp.

"You can't tell me where you come from, can you?" Although her voice is soft, the question makes me tense.

I decide to be truthful, because if I am not, she will know. I shake my head. "I can't." I'm not entirely sure if that's true, yet I've a hunch that I'm not opposed to talking about the caves.

"I see." She smiles. And my chest tightens at the sight of her. It is difficult to keep holding onto the lantern when I keep feeling on the verge of losing myself in her. "Lucina's my name," she shows me another curt nod that finds her hair brushing up against her lithe shoulders. "What's yours?"

I don't want to think about it too long—in fact; I don't think at all. It is as if the stars themselves have blessed me with the name when I blurt, "Atlas." What I'm doing is dangerous. Until today, it was as if I was floating, with no place or body to call home. But now that I have a name, I am more than just a monster, a being to be forgotten in the underground gloom.

Morning swallows the night, over again; over again, the sun bleeds onto the horizon, tangerine waves wash out crepuscular meetings, months pass and I cannot get enough of Lucina, and she cannot get enough of me.

At the break of every few dawns we share stories, breakfast, and she tells me about how the world has changed.

I cannot do it anymore.

I simply cannot.

I cannot continue carrying on as I was, as if I did not exist.

When Lucina invites me inside her home one day, I follow. I know. The lantern's light flickers dimmer with each step I take away from the selenite caves. But I. Cannot help. Myself. I am starved *for her touch.*

I kiss her. On the way there. Beneath pine. When we arrive on her front porch, before a quaint little cottage that could blend into the scenery if one isn't looking hard enough.

The energy here reminds me of the grotto. *Blink and it is gone.* Lucina wraps her arms around my shoulders. She urges me inside, past the doorway. I don't know how many seasons it has been. *Too long* is the only answer that comes to mind. Because I have spent every waking hour dreaming of a life where we are each other's, and everything is right, and I am allowed to adore her without these restraints.

I take Lucina to bed.

I can't explain why I must keep the lantern nearby, but Lucina's made peace with the fact that it's essentially a part of me. And we make love. Past dusk, past midday, until nighttime. And the candle runs out.

I take a breath, expecting it to be my last—yet I do not disappear.

I release the lantern. Run out into the woods.

When I return to the grotto, it has disappeared. I search for it, panting, until the sun rises in the sky and the air is hot. But it is gone.

It is gone. I cannot return, and I am freed in more ways than one. When I glance into the well, I notice my skin has started to age again. *Time is finally elapsing in the rightest of ways.* Under the bluest sky I've ever witnessed, I dash back to the cottage and notice the shape of the monster I once was—an old history—burned into the dark outlines by my feet, that do not match the shape of the man I am today.

Lucina walks out onto the cottage's porch to greet me. As I take her lips with my own and hold her, I catch a glimpse of her shadow in the corner of my eye. It is the same as mine.

NEON NEEDLE
HALLI STARLING

The sign behind the counter read:

- We are a demon and demon-adjacent establishment. We do not tattoo humans.
- No minors. Wait for your horns, claws, teeth, and tails to grow in. Trust us on this one.
- If you're nervous, tell us. You're not a big, tough demon by staying silent and then fainting. Or de-corporalizing. Or turning to dust. Etc, etc.
- There IS a cleaning fee if you sully the rugs. Mabel's very particular about her rugs.
- Finally, we take a 50% deposit when you make your tattoo appointment. We accept any combination of Earth currencies, gems, dragon bones, imp teeth, and petrified eyeballs.
- The eyeballs must be petrified. No exceptions.
- We DO NOT barter. Don't even try it.

When Ilya flicked on the lamp beside her desk, she sighed. The second shift secretary, a nice young achlys named Sweet Before Death, had left a jar of petrified eyes near her computer. The computer's screen kept flickering in response. Technology based on Earth had a tendency to *communicate* with certain things of their realm and her computer screen was putting out some kind of wild story about a machine called a combine and how it didn't just eat fields, but people, too.

And the jar of eyeballs was buying it, hook, line, and sinker.

That would be another rumor she'd have to dispel. Christ on a platter. If she let the computer have its way, it would convert everyone in the office to its strange campaign against land machines. But then again, the computer wanted to be a cult leader and was probably jealous it didn't have wheels or wings, so definitely time to move the eyeballs.

"Okay, boys, girls, thems, theirs, xens, zans, nahns, and so on. No more of this. That computer," and she pointed at the screen, which was now black, "is full of bullshit. You're gonna go in the back and chill with the other eyes."

When the jar didn't protest, Ilya smacked a button under the desk with her claw and waited for the answering beep of the intercom. "Tevondis, can you come up here? Sweet left another jar of eyes out."

"Another? Fuck, that kid."

"I know."

"Shit. How many chances is she on?"

Ilya grimaced. She liked Sweet a lot, but their office manager ran a tight ship and Ilya had already saved her ass a bunch of times. Maybe it was better to let her lose this, so she'd shape up for the next place she worked.

"Admittedly too many. What do I tell Mabel?"

"The truth."

"Well, fuck you, too."

Tevondis laughed, a raspy, growling thing that always warmed her gut. Tevondis had come with the shop, part of the deal Mabel had struck to buy the place for cheap.

Yeah, the building needs some work, but it's got a poppet in the basement no one can evict.

And in true Mabel fashion, they'd asked, *Why the hell would you want to do that? It's her home.*

So Tevondis kept the place running—lights on, fed the fish, kept the eyeballs away from the computer. Most of the time.

Damn. She was really gonna have to call Mabel.

"Ah, shit," Ilya said, reaching for the rotary phone, and Tevondis cackled.

Ilya often fell asleep to the white noise buzz of a tattoo needle. She slept above the shop, and since the place was open all the time, there was always a buzz in the air. How Tevondis was able to transfer all that energy—joy, pain, ecstasy, regret, sorrow— into power for the store … just another mystery. Ilya wasn't one to go poking for answers. Any hole you stuck your head in had at least a one percent chance of cursing or killing you, and neither option was something to fuck around with.

Tonight, though, something bothered her. The buzz was there, on the far side of the store. So, either Jac or 78un was in the shop. Maybe both. Mabel would be floating around downstairs, too. Tevondis would be keeping an ever-vigilant watch from her little nook in the cellar.

Maybe it was the anticipation of having to hire another secretary for second shift. Shit. She'd really thought Sweet had potential, wouldn't have hired her otherwise. A little nervous, sure. A little green. That was fine. Anyone could handle a phone, take notes, put a few entries into the computer. Sweet had come directly from the journeyman's office, so she'd been trained to work this kind of job.

Hmmm.

Another puzzle. She should have been perfect for it.

Dammit.

Unsolved puzzles were like a tag in your shirt, or an errant hair you could feel but couldn't find. It would *pokepokepoke* at her until she unraveled it.

There's no mystery, Ills. Just a young achlys you had to fire today and listen to her sob softly on the phone. And you really should stop calling her kid, she's almost as old as you. You just think anyone younger is automatically inexperienced.

And now she was awake. Moonlight sliced through her windows, illuminating the tank where Marvin, her tarantula, was probably sleeping away. Like she should be.

Her fingers itched to do something. Anything. And then she remembered the pack of cigarettes deep in her nightstand drawer and sighed. So much for kicking the habit. A lounge singer in the 20s had gotten her hooked.

On the cigarettes and on her blonde hair and red lips and touch that felt like fire . . . And it had been fire, she'd been a rather ancient succubus and had been on Earth for literally a millennia.

Ilya slipped into her silk robe and took the fire escape down to the street, not caring that she was about to step outside in a pair of short shorts and a tank top. Anyone who stared at her would get the eyeball. It wasn't like she used that third eye embedded in her forehead much, but being leered at felt like a proper cause.

By the time she was outside in the humid night air, dew sticking to her lizard-smooth skin and making her hair frizz even more, Ilya was glad for those damn cigarettes. She felt on edge in a way that hadn't happened in a while and with no cause, it left her feeling a little adrift. Maybe she could blame it on the jar of eyeballs. They were probably up to something, slimy fucking things. Anything that was buying the computer's wannabe cult nonsense had to be either dense or a master villain.

One cigarette burned up way too fast and soon she was three in, leaning against the wall of the shop, eyes closed, listening to the sounds of neon and needles buzzing through the building.

"Ilya?"

Oh fuck.

Ilya shot up straight, sending her half-finished cigarette flying through the air to land, as if planned, in an oily puddle. She turned and saw Sweet standing at the mouth of the alley, her thin frame wrapped in a frayed tan raincoat. Her wings bunched the back of the coat in an odd, almost disturbing way, folded up as they were, but her tail swung loose, nearly skimming the shining pavement. In the rain and shadows and fuzzy orange sodium light overhead, Sweet's skin looked almost red instead of petal pink.

Sweet was a pretty thing, no doubt about it. But an achlys didn't come into their mesmerism powers until their second century or so, and Sweet was still in her first. So her wide-eyed stare had an almost feline-esque glint as she stepped closer and took in Ilya's outfit. Or lack thereof.

"You trying to give me a heart attack?" Ilya managed to stutter out as she fumbled for her cigarette pack. The robe's pockets were deep and as she fished around, Sweet came closer. Ilya caught the scent of booze. A lot of it.

"No. No. I uh . . . " Sweet swayed, clutched her coat tighter. "I was just out. Walking."

Ilya made a show of sniffing the air. "More than walking."

A giggle. There was a haunting melody under it, something sad and bitter. Sweet couldn't control that snap of power, as drunk as she was. "Turns out I got fired today. Kinda sucks."

Ilya found the cigarettes, pulled them free (sending a few *drachmae* scattering to the slick pavement), and silently offered the pack to the achlys. Sweet frowned, then came close enough to pluck one out. "Thanks."

"Sure." She got Sweet's lit, then her own, and leaned back against the wall. "I'm sorry about that, by the way. Truly."

Sweet mimicked her pose, except she planted one booted foot on the wall and let her head thunk back. The scrape of curled horns against brick sent a shiver down Ilya's spine. "I know. I know you meant it. And I know I'm not right for the job. Just because I trained doesn't mean..." She shook her head. "Never mind."

"We're out here. I can't sleep. Might as well speak your mind."

"Heh." The look Sweet gave her bordered on curiosity. "You were always nice. You and Tevondis, even though she's a grumpy arse."

"Yeah, well..." Ilya inhaled hard, let the smoke curl in her lungs. Her third eye flickered in response and she fought the urge to slap her hand on her forehead in retribution. Damn thing loved it when she smoked. What was with the misbehaving eyes lately? "Everyone kind of just does their own thing, since we all rent our studios. But I was Mabel's first artist to rent one, so I kind of help out where I can." Then she winced, realizing she'd turned the whole thing into a conversation about her feelings. Fuck, she was bad at this. "I know I'm the asshole who fired you, but if I can help…"

The smoke ring Sweet let out lingered in the air, coalescing into something that looked like a lace mandala before being dispersed by the breeze. "It's okay. I don't blame you. Like I said, I was shit at it. And I knew the eyeballs liked talking to the computer, but I didn't pay enough attention." She snorted. "What is that computer doing, by the way?"

"It wants to become a cult leader. And rise up against the wheeled machines.

"No shit." Sweet waved a hand in the air. "Well, good luck with that. If it grows legs, watch out."

They laughed together and it felt nice. She had always liked Sweet but managing her customers, part of the parlor, and the shift secretaries had been too much. Ilya was realizing this now. "Hey."

Sweet opened her eyes. "Hmm?"

"Why did you come back here?"

"Dunno. I was drunk."

"You still are."

"Only a little."

Ilya gave a delicate sniff and realized the scent of rather strong bourbon was nearly gone. "Huh."

"It's an achlys thing. We metabolize pretty much everything really quickly. Especially alcohol. Had to keep up with the Lord of Wine somehow."

"Damn. Lucky."

Sweet laughed again, no girly giggle. But a nice sound, throaty and delighted. "Sorry about my drunken wanderings."

"Don't be." Ilya nudged the achlys with her elbow, an idea forming. "Hey, you want to see something?"

"Ohhhhh." Sweet spun in a slow circle, arms outstretched, raincoat wide open to reveal tight black shorts and a white crop top that rode up under her breasts. The shirt hid absolutely fucking nothing. Ilya forced all three of her eyeballs back into their sockets before handing Sweet a glass of water. "I love this. It's so open."

"Yeah, one of the big reasons why I won't move." Ilya jerked her head toward the front door. "Even with the noise."

"It's not bad. It's almost like those white noise app thingies, to help you sleep." Sweet drained the glass and then set it aside—on a coaster—and shucked off her coat. "Sorry, too warm."

"Hey." Ilya slipped over to her and gently put her hands on Sweet's shoulders. "Stop apologizing."

Sweet blinked those big, shimmering eyes at her and something dropped low in Ilya's stomach. "Okay."

With gentle guidance, Ilya brought Sweet over to her massive drafting desk. "So, I started planning a new set of flash. What do you think?"

She watched as Sweet leaned over the table, taloned hands fluttering over the delicate pieces of paper. They stirred with her breath and movement. "These are *beautiful*, Ilya. They're so lifelike." Sweet pointed to one of Ilya's favorites, a raven with an open beak from which a sprig of holly dangled. "What will it do?"

"I'm leaving that up to whoever gets it done. All of these are like that." She plucked up another one, a delicate line art piece of several wildflowers tied together. "The runes aren't filled in completely, so I can make them do almost anything. Within reason and physics, of course."

"I love it." Sweet's eyes darted over the dozens of pages, but she kept coming back to the raven. "Can I have this one? I have funds for it."

Ilya's gut tightened. Her third eye flickered in anticipation. Damn thing had a *thing* for the achlys. And apparently so did she. Well, shit. "You sure? You ever been tattooed?"

"Nooooo." Sweet shook her head, dark braids flying. Sweet's hair reminded Ilya a little of seaweed, if it was part of some hoarder mermaid's lair. The thick knots were dotted with little flecks of amethyst and topaz, quartz and silver, and in the neon that bled into her apartment from the big bank of windows, Sweet glittered. "But I trust you."

Whew, okay. Ilya had to step back a little, just for some breathing room. She suddenly felt too hot and too cold at the same time, and it was doing *something* to her. Like scrambling her fucking brain. "Well, don't rush the decision. It's not like I'm going anywhere." She waved a clawed hand at their surroundings. "Me and Mabel opened this place. I'll probably die here. Some poor sod will find me mummified in my bed or something."

That got her a look, a keen, peculiar one. One she hadn't expected to weigh so much from someone like Sweet. It never wavered, steadily measuring her against…expectations, perhaps? Outcast gorgons were rare. It was even rarer that an outcast would keep their coils shorn close, with rattles and fangs hacked off and the nubs dipped in hemlock to prevent regrowth. Most outcasts she knew, gorgon or not, went back to their "roots" to feel more at home in their expulsion. But Ilya never felt that way—she'd done it, gotten excised for it, and she never regretted it.

But this was the first time she'd felt seen in the kind of way that made her insides quiver. It wasn't fear, and it wasn't lust. Maybe it was understanding; the kind only creatures like her and Sweet could find together, in a land that wasn't theirs and cut off from anyone back home.

"I don't think that's your fate," Sweet finally said, stepping closer, fingers reaching. Whatever permission she sought, Ilya held it out like an offering before the question could be raised. Maybe it was a little offering, and maybe it was Damocles' fucking sword. "You've been here for, what? Eighty years?"

"Almost ninety." Gods, her throat was dry.

"Almost ninety." Ilya found herself furiously wanting Sweet to touch her, but the achlys denied her. She hovered her hands around Ilya's face, as if framing it, and her defanged, derattled snakes writhed, squirming against her scalp. "I've only been here twenty and it feels like an eternity. Does it get any easier?"

Against the lump in her throat, she said, "It does. It helps finding people. Our people. Other outcasts."

"Hmmm. Then I'm lucky I found you."

She was so close. *So close* that Ilya could breathe her in. That rapid, needy, greedy beast in her wanted something from Sweet but it felt too much, too soon to ask. "If you really want that tattoo…" Sweet's eyes lit up. "We can do it. Now."

"Really?"

Ilya had to laugh at the eagerness. "Yeah, now. Let me get some coffee and we'll go."

"I love your studio." Sweet slowly walked around to take in the art on every surface of Ilya's space. "I know they're all different, and they're all interesting! But yours feels more…homey, in a way. Like this!" She flitted over to the bits of old art in chunky, weathered frames. "This is so cool. Where did you get these frames?"

"Antiques store." When Sweet gave her a confused look, Ilya chuckled. "I'll take you sometime. Humans have this knack for keeping old shit in their houses, then reselling it or giving it away when someone in their family dies."

Sweet looked aghast. "They give away family heirlooms?"

"Ah, well…kind of? Sometimes? It's not like back home, where we keep things like blood vials and altars. Humans collect *a lot* of shit over their short lives. They like to make their homes look nice and when they die, it's not all valuable pieces that people want to keep." She gestured to the frames. "So the stuff winds up in these stores full of weird, cool things and you can buy them."

"Huh. Like a . . . mausoleum of stuff from all kinds of people."

"Except these places charge and you don't walk away with stone dust in your nostrils." Ilya snapped rubber gloves onto her hands and said, "Okay, I'm ready if you are. Show me where you want it?"

With a graceful hop into the chair, Sweet stuck out her muscular right leg and pointed at her thigh. She was already wearing shorts cut high enough that Ilya could work around them, but she didn't want to get the achlys's clothes dirty. "So sometimes ink will get onto clothes. I can give you something from my closet—"

But Sweet was already back up and shimmying out of faded black shorts before Ilya could turn away. She should have figured Sweet wasn't shy; most achlyses weren't in general. And the crop top and shorts she had on underneath that demure raincoat hadn't been a *shock*, per se. But Ilya had lived in the slightly gray, foggy spaces around the human world long enough that some of their peculiarities were maybe rubbing off on her. With a simple glamour and the right clothes, she could easily walk among them. And Sweet could learn to do that, too, given time and experience. But she had no qualms like them, worried about their bodies and what others would think of them, and it made some part of Ilya ache again with *want*.

"Okay well . . . " Ilya laid down more of the crinkly paper to keep ink off her chair, and to keep Sweet's bare ass from sticking to the seat. Because the achlys was wearing a tiny pair of boy shorts and all that bare skin would definitely stick. That was her only concern. Absolutely.

Once Sweet was settled back in the chair, Ilya sat down on her stool. Sweet showed her exactly where to place the tattoo and she got to work, tracing the stenciling runes, activating the little well of enhanced ink, and finally taking a few sips of coffee. "Ready?"

"Totally." Sweet grinned at her, all fangs and plum-wine lips. "I'm practicing my human. How is it?"

The little wiggle Sweet gave made Ilya grit her teeth. Fuck. "It's good."

"Yay!"

"Ready?"

"Yes." All goofy pretense dropped from Sweet's face and she reached up to touch the gems and teeth dangling from her right horn. "How bad will it hurt?"

"Well," Ilya said as she sat back, glad for the extra moment to breathe but wishing Sweet had asked this *before* her ass had hit the chair, "you picked a spot with a lot of muscle and one not close to the bone, so it's about as good as it can be for a first time. If you'd picked along your spine," and Sweet hissed, which made her nod, "then I might have double-triple checked you were sure. But once we get going, the pain will subside. Plus it won't take long, maybe thirty minutes. And then we can set the runes and wait for them to finish writing."

"Ooooh, okay. Then yes, let's."

Ilya flipped the switch to her machine, put her right hand on the inside of Sweet's thigh (*professional professional be professional*), and paused, pulsing neon needle high in the air. "Ready?"

Sweet's grin was wide and honest. "Totally."

Sweet chose to have the raven blink and the sprig of holly sway. Nothing too crazy for a first tattoo, and Ilya was grateful for it. She could feel her energy waning as she cleaned up Sweet's leg and put away her gear; and since setting the runes was always tiring, the ease of the achlys's request helped to.

When she packed away her obsidian wood and taramite wand, the air still buzzed with magical energy. Sweet was looking down at her tattoo with an expression of soft awe when Ilya turned back around. "You okay?"

"Yes. Very much so. I love it, Ilya. It's beautiful."

"Glad you like it." She gestured to the ceiling. "We can wait in my apartment while the runes finish, if you want. You might be more comfortable there."

The grin she got in response was cheeky. It made something twitch low in her belly, that grin. "Should I leave my shorts off?"

"Uh. I mean. I don't know."

"You're the expert."

Her brain completely shorted out. "No idea, up to you."

Sweet just laughed and shimmied back into her shorts and then waited for Ilya to shut the studio down. Her companion was silent on the short walk back upstairs, and by the time Ilya had the door unlocked, Sweet was too preoccupied with staring down at her leg, turning it this way and that, to notice Ilya had gone quiet.

While she rummaged around the kitchen, looking for something to offer her guest, she missed Sweet slipping in beside her at the tiny kitchen island. "So, can I give you a hug? As a thank you?"

Oh, she was so close. Too close. Ilya could smell her skin and the soft musk of her horns, wanted to feel their suede nubs under her fingertips. "You already paid me," she said weakly, not trusting her control if she caught Sweet's gaze in her own.

"Oh, sorry. Yeah, you're right—"

Sweet turned away and Ilya didn't stop herself. Couldn't stop herself. She caught Sweet's wrist, feeling the delicate bones shift. Heard the other woman's quiet gasp. "I didn't say no. I'm deflecting," she admitted, finally letting herself look the achlys in the eye. Those glittering voids were wide with wonder, burgundy lips dropped open in delighted shock. "I don't touch a lot of . . . anyone, really. Even a lot of outcasts are too worried I'll turn them to stone."

"That's fucking stupid." Sweet's face was a mask of righteous fury and Ilya marveled at how every emotion she felt was written proudly across high, sculpted cheekbones. Even Sweet's tattered, dark purple wings were fluttering in agitation.

Ilya shrugged. "Can't dispel some myths, I guess."

"Still fucking stupid."

"Thanks."

"So…"

She wasn't about to quash the woman's need or desire for a hug now. "Yeah. A hug would be nice. Sorry, again."

But Sweet's little smile turned flirty and oh no, that feeling of *need* was flaring hot in her again. Godsdammit. "Okay but…I was gonna ask if I could kiss you after the hug, so whoops, spoiled it."

And she just had to run her big mouth. "I fired you," she protested weakly, not stopping Sweet from steering them back. Back. Back one more time, until Ilya's shoulders hit the wall. Those finely boned hands with sharp, sharp nails landed on either side of her head and her snakes —traitors, the lot of them—hissed in satisfaction. "What are you doing?"

"Kissing you."

"Oh."

"Yes?"

Ilya nodded. Sweet kissed her with the care and attention only an achlys could give, and all Ilya tasted was candy.

Sweet Before Death. The name made sense now. She thought it was some warrior-esque name worthy of Artemis or Diana, but Sweet delivered her own kind of death. Slowly, with plum-wine lips and delicate hands and the ozone-spark of rain.

"Oy, love birds. The computer's gone."

Tevondis's crackly voice echoed through Ilya's apartment. She pried her eyes open, gaze landing on the water spots on the ceiling. Beside her, Sweet was curled up like a kitten and snoring adorably. Ilya was pretty sure she never, ever wanted to move again.

"Ignoring me is only going to end badly. I control the building, remember?"

"Fuckin' hell," Ilya mumbled, then cleared her throat to say, "Yeah, I hear you. What do you mean the computer's gone?"

That got Ilya a rusty laugh, reminding her of the old needles they'd plucked out of a molding drawer when Mabel had first bought the place. It seemed the building's fate had long been to house body modifications of all sorts, from piercings and tattoos to more extreme notions involving scalloped skin and sandpaper-esque hooks for grinding and smoothing. All of that had freaked Mabel out a tad, but since then, Tevondis liked to make her laugh sound like those tools, just a little. Mostly to piss Mabel off, and somewhat because the poppet couldn't help but mimic noises she found interesting.

"Grew legs and walked off, for all I know," Tevondis replied. "Woke up, went to start the coffee before Mabel came in, and saw no computer at the front desk and only a weird trail of something kind of viscous leading to the kitchenette."

Sweet snuffled closer to Ilya and she wrapped an arm around the achlys's narrow shoulders. "Wouldn't the cameras have caught that?"

"No cameras, love. The footage fizzled out at exactly the right time."

"What? Shit, Mabel's gonna lose it."

A sound not unlike a train whistle came from downstairs. "Think she's already on her way there. Better get a hustle on, Ils."

"Ah, fuck. Shit. Fuck." Ilya flew across her apartment to throw on clean clothes and high tops before practically launching herself at the bed to nudge Sweet. "Hey, hot stuff. I gotta go downstairs. You stay and sleep, okay."

"Mmmkay."

Ilya had to chuckle at that before planting a kiss on Sweet's forehead and booking it down to the shop's main floor. That train whistle noise sounded again and Ilya winced as she slammed through the back door leading to the kitchenette to find Mabel squeezing the life out of a stress ball, steam coming out of her ears.

"The fuck is this?" Mabel cried, making the stress ball's eyes bulge out disturbingly. She pointed a metal-jointed finger to the slime trail across the floor, then at the strange purple and green fleshy sac on the wall to the left of the small bank of chipped cabinets. "Ilya?"

"Ew." Ilya leaned forward to get a better look. She was hit with a smell not unlike wet mushrooms nestled in moss, and while it wasn't *unpleasant*, Ilya did not want to know what was in the thing undulating gently on the wall. "Mabel, I have no idea. I just woke up."

The woman's mechanical eyes narrowed at her. "Get rid of it, then. Just . . . ugh. We are not taking payments in eyeballs anymore. Fucking things."

Ilya stayed rooted to the floor. "I am not touching that."

Mabel frowned, seeming to realize what she was asking for was *not* in Ilya's work contract. "Okay, then…call an exterminator. Haven't we tattooed a few of them in all these years?"

The sac shifted, made a gurgling noise, then burped. Something clattered to the floor. Ilya just stared at it. "Is that a *computer chip*?"

Mabel's mouth opened in horror. "Oh no. OH NO. Absolutelyfuck-ingnotgetthatthingoutofhere!"

Sweet chose that moment to bounce into the room in Ilya's black silk robe saying, "Hey Ilya, your coffee maker got mad at me. Is there—holy shit."

"I think," Ilya said slowly, putting her arm out to push Sweet back into the hall, "the computer and the jar of eyeballs are uh . . . . reproducing."

"Absolutely fucking NOT IN MY STORE!" Mabel screeched, her voice going all train whistle once more.

Below their feet, Tevondis let out a cackle. "I told y'all those eyeballs were bad news!"

Sweet helped her make a new sign. Ilya hung it up, got Mabel's thumbs-up approval, and stepped back. Sweet hooked an arm around her waist and grinned up at her. "I think I should hire out my handwriting skills. What do you think?"

The hot pink paint was impossible to miss, especially in Sweet's neat-as-pie handwriting. "I think you might have a spot as a hand letterer in the shop," Ilya said, earning her a smacking kiss to her cheek. "Seriously. It's really good. Work on some lettering samples and we can talk."

"Oh my god!"

Mabel leaned in, squinting at them both. "Didn't Ilya fire you, kid?"

Sweet's lightly scaled cheek ridges went dark red, which Ilya thought was pretty fucking adorable. "Yes, but—"

"Yeah, yeah." Mabel pointed at Ilya, finger joint creaking slightly. "Same rules apply. You hire, you fire, but if she's working in your booth, there's an extra fee I'm tacking onto your monthly rent."

Ilya wasn't worried. A hand letterer would be good for the entire shop, not just her spot, and she could convince the others to hire Sweet. Most of the artists in Neon Needle hated doing lettering, and Sweet *was* really good.

"Fine by me," Ilya said, squeezing Sweet to her side. Mabel huffed and wheeled off, leaving them alone before the new sign. "We'll work something out, won't we?"

Sweet beamed up at Ilya, tail curling around one of Ilya's calves. "You bet your ass."

When Ilya wanted to dip out for lunch a few hours later, she caught Sweet at the front desk, filing her talons and chatting with the new assistant. "I've heard the phone ringing all morning. Been handling it okay, Ivan?"

"It's. Been. Fine." Ivan said, giving Ilya a stiff wave. "Enjoy. Your. Lunch."

"Bye, Ivan!" Sweet called as she skipped ahead to hold open the door for Ilya. "My lady."

Ilya snickered. "Why, thank you."

They walked hand in hand down the street and around the corner to the little cafe Ilya knew had the best Reubens. "So, how's Ivan handling his first day?"

"Pretty good." Sweet slipped on her sunglasses and wrinkled her nose against the sun's heat. "I'm kinda surprised Mabel let an automaton work for the shop. I thought when she said no machines, she meant *no machines*."

Ilya had been wondering when this would come up. No daytime assistant in the store was a nightmare for all of them, and no matter how much Sweet offered to help, Mabel kept insisting they just needed to wait for the new guy to start. Ivan *was* efficient from the get-go, and seemed tireless, so she supposed that was a point in his favor.

"Well, she's not gonna say it, but that automaton is her nephew."

Sweet paused mid-step, and slowly let her combat booted foot fall to the ground. "Damn."

Ilya shrugged, grinning. Automatons were really rare outside their home plane, and most disguised their voice and appearance with magic. Mabel giving her nephew a position in her shop was not only the safest thing she could do for him, it was also a giant middle finger to Ivan's home, which was rather well-known for being run by an oppressive regime. "That's Mabel for you. She's outcast just like I am. Jac fled their father's kingdom about two hundred years ago. Mabel's real good at collecting outsiders and giving them a home."

"Damn," Sweet said again, this time far softer. "Well, shit. I just thought she was a hardass. I should know better than to judge folks." Her tail wound around Ilya's wrist. "Which, by the way, thank you for not judging me too much when you had to fire me."

Ilya could only smile. Sweet looked so open and earnest and it made Ilya want to kiss it right off her mouth. "Hey, like I said, Mabel's good at collecting outcasts. It turns out you just needed to find your reason to be outcast."

"From the shop?" Sweet huffed but it was all hot air. "Rude."

"Yep. But it was only once. It was the test you had to pass."

"To do what?"

Ilya ruffled Sweet's hair and when Sweet looked up, she leaned in for a kiss. "To become family."

The new sign above the door—and on the now computer-less desk read:

- We are a demon and demon-adjacent establishment. We do not tattoo humans.
- No minors. Wait for your horns, claws, teeth, and tails to grow in. Trust us on this one.
- If you're nervous, tell us. You're not a big, tough demon by staying silent and then fainting. Or de-corporalizing. Or turning to dust. Etc., etc.
- There IS a cleaning fee if you sully the rugs. Mabel's very particular about her rugs.
- Finally, we take a 50% deposit when you make your tattoo appointment. We accept any combination of Earth currencies, gems, dragon bones, and imp teeth.
- We DO NOT barter. Don't even try it.
- We are a paper-based store for all records. We thank you for your patience.

And at the bottom in very large, bold letters, it read:

- ABSOLUTELY NO EYEBALLS ALLOWED. NO JARS, SACRIFICIAL BOWLS, VIALS, FREEZER BAGS, COOLERS, ETC. IF YOU DO, THE POPPET IN THE BASEMENT WILL USE YOU FOR TARGET PRACTICE.

ABOUT THE AUTHORS

Rita A. Rubin is an award-winning author who currently resides in Melbourne and is living her best introvert life. When not writing, Rita can be found with her nose in a book, or PS4 console in her hands or making up ballads to sing to her dog and cat.

Nicole Tota is an author of sapphic speculative fiction whose creative works can be found in Broken Olive Branches, Polyphony Lit Magazine, and Forest for the Trees, among others. She is the founder of #QueerPit, a Twitter pitch contest dedicated to matching LGBTQ+ writers with agents. When not writing, she can be found snuggling with her two foster fail cats and tackling her endless TBR pile.

Taylor Hubbard is a transmasc man who focuses on writing queer stories of all varieties. He enjoys hanging out with his cats, listening to 2000s emo music, and chugging as many energy drinks as humanly possible.

Talli L. Morgan is the author of The Windermere Tales series and several other fantasy novels. When they're not writing, Talli enjoys playing D&D, drawing, and flinging book recommendations at unsuspecting library patrons. Visit them at tallimorgan.com.

Dewi Hargreaves is an author, editor and illustrator from the cold, soggy middle of the UK. His short fiction has been published by Etherea Magazine and others, and his flash piece 'Maccabeus' came 2nd in Grindstone Literary's Open Prose Competition 2017.

Amanda Ferreira works in publishing, as an editor. She lives in Toronto with her tuxedo cat, Milo, and when not writing, can be found baking, running, listening to a true crime podcast, or working on a cosplay.

Mawce Hanlin is a non-binary, autistic author who writes stories about found family, self-love, and queer/disabled acceptance.

Aimee Donnellan is a bisexual indie author based in New Zealand, who writes whimsical fantasy stories full of adventure and romance. When not writing, she can be found playing D&D or video games.

Beau Van Dalen is a best-selling author of adult speculative fiction. Published by Tapas Media and Radish, Wattpad Stars Alumnus and Winner of Tapas's 2018 Summer Writing Competition—Beau's stories have amassed over one million reads online. Beau is always enchanting words and creating worlds, he is currently on a journey to publish one-hundred novels.

Halli Starling has always been involved with books, and her love of the written word inspired her to get her Master's in Library Science and continue her book career outside of public libraries. When not writing, she co-hosts *The Human Exception* podcast, plays D&D, and spends time in the beautiful outdoors of Michigan.